PREHISTORIC WWII

DANE HATCHELL

SEVERED PRESS
HOBART TASMANIA

PREHISTORIC WWII

CHAPTER 1

May 4, 1945. The USS Sutton, a Cannon-class Destroyer of the US Navy, cruised the blue waters of the Bermuda operation area for her shakedown. Once proven battle-worthy, it was full speed ahead to end the "Good War" in Europe.

Captain T.W. Brazo held the 7X50 powered binoculars above his well-groomed chevron mustache as he scanned the rolling North Atlantic Ocean. Because the war had resources limited, the binoculars were part of a national program asking citizens, *Will You Supply Eyes for the Navy?* A tag indicated the charitable owner's name and address. The Navy wasn't authorized to accept gifts, so a single dollar was paid as a token of appreciation. Still, the president promised the return, if possible, of all the binoculars once the war ended. Brazo had read over fifty thousand citizens responded.

The war in Europe brought many hardships to the American people. As bad as the depression had hit, crippling the country to an all-time low, Americans didn't lose faith in freedom when faced with the rise of the Axis powers. The United States was founded on the stance of, *Give me liberty or give me death.* Those were just words, though. The proof came in the actions of hundreds of thousands of men and women who sacrificed their lives in pursuit of liberty. Not just for the United States, but for all freedom-loving people of the world.

The wind blew calmly, caressing his cheeks. The smell of the salty ocean spray carried all the way up to the observation deck. A crewman busily worked on an assigned task on deck.

Brazo loved everything about the ocean. His earliest memory was cooling his heels in Cocoa Beach with his mom holding one hand and his dad the other. Most of his friends liked playing with toy trucks or *cowboys and Indians*. Not him. He preferred dressing up as a pirate and becoming a scourge of the Seven Seas. His favorite toys were miniature ships and boats. A long stick for a sword and a rag tied over one eye transformed him into the infamous *Captain Black Brazo*. The Jolly Roger hung proudly above his bed, threatening any monsters who crept into his room during the night that it would be they who would be the victim.

The Executive Officer, Captain Alan Slick, referred to as XO so as to not confuse his rank with the commander of the ship, stepped from the top of the ladder to the observation deck. "Captain," he said, stiffening to attention for a moment.

"Slick, come up to the crow's nest for some fresh air? Can't blame you. Those beans served at lunch may be Hitler's latest secret weapon. Imagine, asphyxiating nearly three-hundred men by their own farts, and not a shot fired."

"I wouldn't put anything past the Nazis, sir. But the way the war is going for them, I suspect they'd eat the beans to do themselves in."

"They might at that," Brazo said, continuing to scan the horizon.

Slick turned his attention toward the ocean, lifted his cap, and ran his fingers through his coarse black hair. "Do you believe the reports are true? That Hitler committed suicide? I know that news is something I *want* to believe."

"Hard to say," Brazo said, gazing toward the XO. "There's the rumor that his body was cremated, too. Without any hard evidence, we can't be sure. This is no time for us to let our guard down. We're making progress, but if the Nazis get that so-called *atomic bomb* before we do, it won't matter if Hitler's running the show or not."

"If there's a God, that won't happen."

"If there's a God, the damned war wouldn't have happened," Brazo said, his tone filled with his disgust for the inhuman atrocities committed by the Nazis on innocent people. He understood war, even perpetrated from crazed dictators who wanted to dominate the world. What he didn't understand was genocide, or torturing people and treating them worse than animals. Cracks in the Nazi propaganda revealed the Jews not being cared for in the detention camps as portrayed on short films. No children's opera or clean, comfortable living quarters. No abundance of tasty and nutritious food. The reality was far darker than the fantasy. The detainees actually had been transformed into something almost not recognizable as human. Starvation created near-walking skeletons. Eyes stared death-like from blackened, sunken sockets. Pure instinct the only power driving the day-to-day survival.

"I'm not trying to debate the existence of God, again," Slick said. "I just know I have to believe a greater power will come to the side of good when the consequences are so great."

"It's a matter of wills. Human wills. But, I'll at least grant you I do believe the power of good is stronger than the power of evil. The human spirit is the hardest fire to extinguish. The will to live…to be free, is stronger than all the Gods combined," Brazo said, not wanting the philosophical discussion to grow any further. "How's the *shakedown* going? The aft engines seem to be running smoother today."

"They are. The electricians adjusted the cycle on one of the diesel engines to sync with the electric drive. The major problems were corrected a week ago. The way it looks now, I think we'll be heading across the ocean before the end of the month." Slick paused a moment, and said, "Uh, there're a couple of things, though. The radio, we can receive but can't transmit. The problem reared its head around the same time some interference on the radar screen showed up. Probably bad tubes."

"What kind of interference?"

"A huge blob of green started darkening the screen in one corner."

"What direction?"

"To the southwest."

Brazo spun and walked over to the other side of the observation deck. The bright blue sky was slowly encroached by billowing clouds strange in color. He lifted the binoculars and focused. "Hmm."

"What, sir?" Slick asked, stepping up behind him.

"Those aren't ordinary clouds out there. They hang from the sky all the way down to the water and…and they're green."

"I've seen *green* clouds before. Right before a tornado touched down on our farm. But I have to admit, nothing like those over there."

The captain of a ship knows to respect the weather. Even the mightiest of vessels can be tossed about and crushed under Neptune's tantrums. Thunderstorms he could handle, especially knowing he was only twenty miles from base. But for some reason this cloud formation had his *gut feeling* twisting his insides. Brazo had learned to trust his instincts. Why *spit into the wind if you don't have to*? "I think it would be in our best interest if we headed back to base. I realize that there's zero chance we'll be attacked out here from the air. But what if it's not *just a tube* affecting the radar? There might be a larger electrical problem growing. Let's avoid the bad weather and head back to the base."

"Yes, sir. You're the captain," Slick said. The man turned to leave when the observation deck radio squawked.

"Captain? Over," the voice of Jim Stone said.

Brazo strode over and grabbed the mic. "Brazo. Go ahead, over."

"Radar's picked up a bogey two miles starboard. We suspect it's a periscope."

"Are you sure? XO Slick tells me the radar is on the blink," Brazo said.

"The radar screen not affected by the interference appears to be one hundred percent functional. Something's definitely out there."

"U-boat, sir?" Slick asked. "We've been whopping the hell out of them over the last several months. Wouldn't expect to find a straggler out here outside of a major shipping lane."

"Intel says influential Nazis are fleeing like rats to South America. It wouldn't surprise me if some of the bloodiest Krauts ever to goosestep were aboard that can." Brazo narrowed his gaze.

His fingers turned white as he squeezed the binoculars hanging by his chest. "I can't let my emotions get in the way of the safety of this ship or my men. You're my XO. This ship is not officially commissioned to engage the enemy. But give me one reason why we shouldn't go after it."

Slick's stoic expression hid any emotion as he paused to calculate the risks. "I can't, sir. All weapons are operational."

"And the storm to the southwest? The U-boat is heading straight for it."

"Let's make it the Jerry's last voyage. It always rains at funerals, and it never rains in Hell."

A slight grin curled from the left side of Brazo's mouth. "Let's put some *fun* in this funeral." He pushed the mic's button. "This is Captain Brazo. Battle stations!"

CHAPTER 2

Lieutenant Commander Christoph Neuzetser pressed his face against the U-boat periscope's eye shield as he struggled to focus on the approaching Destroyer. It greatly annoyed him that age had degraded the fine-tuned machine he once was and threatened to put him on an equal level of his inferior enemies. He was only forty-five years old. Growing up, his father never told him how a man's body changed as he aged. He might understand if he were in his sixties, certainly in his seventies. But forty-five?

Perhaps it was stress. Something a member of the Nazi SS was sure to live with but never allowed to admit. The doctor had suggested stress affected the eyes' performance and issued him eyeglasses; something he would use only to read with—and mostly when he wasn't in view of others. He was the commander, a representative of the feared *Kriegsmarine*, not a cripple. Christoph would lead without curved glass filtering the fire of his ice-blue eyes.

The twin diesel engines growled incessantly as *U-616* cruised beneath the waters of the North Atlantic. Faint aromatic petrol fumes permeated the air. Everything in the submarine's compartments had a slightly oily feel. Shaving and showers were land luxuries not afforded to submariners.

"Destroyer...Cannon class. Three kilos...one point abaft starboard beam," Christoph said.

"Alone?" Lt. Gunter Bach asked. Though ten years younger than Christoph, the gray peppering his dark beard made him look older.

"Yes. Definitely alone."

"A Cannon class should be escorting merchant ships, not roaming the ocean."

"We are not far from a shipyard. Perhaps this one is on its maiden voyage and will present us no harm." Christoph had both wrists resting on the periscope's turn handles. He stepped a slow 360° while straining to focus across the endless waters. No other vessels in sight. "We are heading straight for a storm."

"The storm is interfering with the radar. I've never seen anything like this," Ensign Otto Faulk said, seated at his station.

Problems with the radar were something they didn't need right now. His left foot stepped in something wet. His boot smeared a swatch of grime across the floor. Christoph looked over in the corner of the command room. His son, Erik, held his head low, sulking.

Part of Christoph wanted to grab Erik by the shoulders, give him a good shake, and slap him back into reality, saying, *The German youth fights for the Führer and the people.* The war with the Allies was sure to be lost, but the war Germans fought every day of their life, to be a proud and superior race, would go on. World War I threatened Germany's survival. Even though they had lost *The Great War*, the Aryan race, mainly through the leadership of the Führer, rose from the ashes to near world domination. *One, all it takes is one person to change the course of history*, he had often told Erik. Christoph wanted only the best for his son and for him to be head and shoulders above the elite.

The other part of Christoph wanted to hug his son tightly and let Erik know he understood the severe grief he felt. Allied bombing had killed Gerda, Erik's mother, only three weeks before. Losing his wife had been tough on Christoph too but in a different way. A very different way. The war had separated them for years. Even before the war, their relationship had become strained. Learning of her death brought great sadness. Not so much for losing their future together, but for losing what *should have been* but never was from the beginning.

It was much harder for a fifteen-year-old boy to lose his mother than a man estranged from his wife.

"Erik," Christoph said, authority in his voice, waiting for his son to look his way. His call passed through the room with no effect. "Son, fetch a tool bag from the engine room. A flange from a ballast tank is leaking."

A round-faced officer from the SS Security Service, with a finely chiseled nose and strong chin, stepped just to the entrance of the airlock into the command room. He hesitated to enter farther, not calling attention to himself. The officer was either being polite or was spying. SS officers weren't known for politeness. His hand dropped alongside his chest, a glowing cigarette between his fingers.

Erik slowly lifted his gaze through drooping eyelids. His expression hid whether he hadn't understood the request or if it was a task he had decided not to do.

Christoph stepped away from the periscope. He motioned his head to the side, signaling Bach to take his place. "If you are in my command room you must make yourself useful. We don't need bodies taking space. Get some tools and tighten the flange, or leave and help the cook in the galley. You earned a ribbon shooting targets with a Mauser in Youth Camp. I am sure you are skilled enough to peel a potato." Christoph regretted his condescending words as soon as they left his lips. He didn't want to embarrass the boy, only inspire him. It certainly didn't come out that way.

Erik slowly shook his head, the spark of life dim in his eyes. "If I leave or stay doesn't matter to me. Wherever I go, life is the same. I am still in a boat. I am no longer in the Fatherland. My home is gone. My leader is dead. My mother is dead. My country has lost the war." His bottom lip rose and quivered. "My country is *dead*."

"Hold your tongue!" Christoph said. His hand was forced, now was the time. He had to set his son on a path that would save or utterly destroy him. With a raised finger, Christoph pointed, face reddening, and a growing snarl curling his lips. Before he could release Armageddon, Bach interrupted.

"Commander, the Destroyer is turning on an interception course. We are discovered."

Emotions had distracted Christoph from his duties as commander. A US Destroyer, designed specifically for submarine warfare, threatened his final mission. The most important mission in his life. The *U-616* carried drawings, arms, medical supplies, instruments, lead, mercury, caffeine, steels, optical glass, and brass. There was secret cargo too. Two short tonnes of uranium oxide designated for the nuclear project hid away. But the most precious cargo, the primary purpose of this mission, was getting a select few out of Germany, out of the hands of the Allies, and brought safely to Brazil.

Christoph looked at the man who shadowed the airlock's entrance, Klaus Barbie. A member of the Gestapo, he had earned the nickname of *The Butcher of Lyon*. The commander didn't know how much truth was in the rumors concerning the cruelty of this man, but he could feel the coldness of his presence between them. "Captain Barbie, please inform the other guests and our two patients of the situation."

The glowing tip of Barbie's cigarette smoldered.

Christoph wasn't a fan of tobacco, but he was thankful others were. The smell of cigarettes was more desirable than the body odors, mildew funk, and battery and machinery fumes ever present in a U-boat.

"Erik, go with the captain and make yourself useful. Make sure the patients are comfortable," Christoph said.

Barbie mashed the fading glow of his smoke on a callused palm. He left without saying a word. He didn't need to speak; the commander knew what was at stake.

"Even if we surface, we can't outrun them," Christoph said. "This is our final mission. Our duty is to ensure it is the Destroyer's last mission too."

CHAPTER 3

"He's turning, sir!" Jim Sone called from his station.

The U-boat had been heading straight into the radar screen's blob of interference, where it was sure to be lost. Whether it was fortunate for the *Sutton's* crew to engage the enemy, only time would tell.

"All right, every man to his duties," Brazo yelled from the command room. "Full speed ahead. Prepare the torpedo launchers on deck and wait for them to come out of the turn. Have the hedgehogs on the ready, and fire within distance without my command. *Fight 'til she sinks, boys*!" He ended his order with a battle cry he plagiarized from Captain James Lawrence, USN, 1813.

The U-boat was taking them head on, which was an aggressive move for a single vessel to make. The German captain must either be crazy or that confident. U-boats were known for attacking in packs, known as *wolf packs*. Submarines were best suited for ambushing naval vessels. This would be no game of hide and seek.

If the torpedoes didn't find their target, then the *hedgehogs* surely would. Brazo had the utmost confidence in the forward-throwing anti-submarine weapon. Twenty-four spigot mortars launched toward the sub would land in a circular pattern. The heavy projectiles would sink so fast they would be two hundred feet down in nine seconds. Unlike depth charges, which relied on pressure or time switches to detonate, and shockwaves to do damage, the mortar projectiles had contact fuses. Detonation always occurred directly against the sub's hull. One or two direct hits was sufficient to take out the enemy.

"He's completed the turn," Stone said. "It's a good thing. The radar interference is almost on top of both of us."

"Launch the torpedoes," Brazo said. The *Sutton* had four launchers on deck. Two Mark 14 torpedoes would fly at first volley. The undersea missiles had their flaws. Some had run ten feet deeper than set. The magnetic exploder often fired prematurely, and the contact exploder often failed to engage. It had been documented that some torpedoes had gone awry, turned, and circled back to hit the firing ship. This was 1945, though. Naval brass assured him most of the problems had been corrected.

*

The forward main battery director, Robert Lucas, barked orders to the helmsman. The massive hunk of steel gliding the waters turned to allow the torpedo tubes unobstructed access to its target. Two crewmen atop the tubes sighted the enemy.

The strange green clouds in the distance rolled in faster than he'd ever seen before. What kind of storm was this? It was as if an ethereal void quickly consumed both ocean and sky. His heart pounded faster. The small hairs on the back of his neck prickled. Inside his station, everything became electrified.

*

"Sonar has two torpedoes heading forward," Stone said. "And...." Popping noises and glass shattering came from inside his console. He lurched forward in his seat, methodically twisting knobs. "Sir, radar and sonar just stopped working."

"Damnit! Inform the helmsman. Evasive Action," Brazo commanded. The words he spoke dropped in volume in his head. Electricity crawled up and down his back. Others must have felt it, too. Everyone had frozen in position and looked bewilderingly about.

The overhead lights went out. The engine hum stopped. The *Sutton* was dead in the water.

*

The two crewmen on top of the torpedo launcher looked curiously at each other. The green fog surrounded them, limiting visibility to only three or four feet.

"What the hell is this? What do we do?" Pratt, the larger of the two, asked.

"I didn't have time to sight in the torpedoes. If we launch them now they're sure to miss," Cummings said.

"Crap! Crap! Crap!" Pratt stood and put his hands on either side of his sailor's cap. "There's a sub heading for us. We've got to find it. It's our job to shoot it. We're gonna die. We're gonna die!"

"Get ahold of yourself, man! Acting like a mama's boy ain't gonna save our hides. Get your ass back over here. Just as the fog lifts, we'll be ready. There's nothing else for us to do. There…." Cummings words lodged in his throat, refusing to escape his mouth. Something reddish in color emerged from the green mist. It was shaped blade-like and had the width of three men. Suction cups the size of beach balls dripped with the ocean's briny liquid. An aquatic funk rolled in as Pratt's outburst subsided.

Water dripped onto Pratt's shoulders. His mouth dropped open, reading the fear on Cumming's face. His upper lip rose as there was no escaping the strange odor. He slowly turned his head, eyes bulging at the horrific sight.

The giant squid's feeding tentacle collapsed around Pratt's body. Fear became his master, and a high-pitched squeal emanated from his throat. Round, quivering suckers mashed against his skin like soft, wet rubber. Pratt struggled, but he was held fast in the grip of a prehistoric cephalopod. The tentacle plucked him off the launcher.

The green fog sluggishly lifted, and Cummings watched as the tentacle slid across the steel deck with its prisoner. "Pratt! Pratt!" Screaming his mate's name did nothing to stop the slow descent to certain death.

Finding his legs, Cummings climbed down the launcher and ran toward Pratt. The tentacle slithered backward, nearing the ship's edge.

"Cummings!" Pratt cried. His right arm free, he stretched out his hand, clawing empty air for an invisible hold.

"I'll save you, buddy!" Cummings streaked over and grabbed onto Pratt's right wrist.

Pratt similarly latched onto his, and the battle was on.

Cummings felt Pratt's fingernails dig into his forearm. He brought his left hand over to double his grip, planted his feet as firmly on the deck as possible, and strained with all his might. He might as well have been pulling against a bulldozer.

A sucker had Pratt's left cheek in its vicious clasp. It pulled at skin, stretching it away from his skull. He yelled out in agony as the rest of his body suffered as if his blood was being sucked out through his flesh.

Cummings dragged along until his body touched the deck's rail. He put all of his remaining strength into one final tug as he came to a momentary solid halt.

The sucker tugged so greatly against Pratt's face that his left eye popped out the socket. The bloodshot orb dangled, oddly swaying like a grandfather clock pendulum bob, connected to the skull by the optic nerve. He disappeared over the rail.

Cummings, still holding on, felt his feet leave the deck.

*

The emergency lights came on in the command room, giving enough light to quickly let the crew know how screwed they were.

"Get those engines back on, now!" Brazo felt like a one-winged duck in a pond surrounded by hunters. "Weapons report. We need to fire torpedoes as quick as we can."

"Radio's out, sir," Slick said, the microphone clutched in his hand.

"Damnit! I'll fire those things myself." As Brazo turned to leave, an explosion rocked the ship from underneath, sending him sideways. Before he righted himself, the second explosion sent him to his knees. A few seconds later, a bright flash in the command center and a crack of thunder blinded him, setting his ears ringing.

*

Unseen hands clamped down on Cummings' legs as he nearly spilled over the deck. Pratt was in the unbreakable grasp of the giant squid. Cummings felt Pratt's arm slip away forever, the warmth of life pulsing from his lost mate replaced by the cool dampness of ocean spray.

"My gosh...look," one of the three crewmen who came to Cummings' rescue said.

The squid's stabilizing fin and mantle rose from the water, resembling a mountain shaped like the Devil's horn. Its reddish skin glistened in the emerging sunlight, the green clouds and fog rapidly dissipating. The beast looked like something from another world. No, something more than that. A God. A being so powerful, so fearful, that nothing on Earth could be its equal.

Its single eye left the deep, and the mighty creature floated as high as the ship's two smokestacks. The eye had the power to peer directly into a man's soul and slowly sip out his will to live.

Pratt silently thrashed about, either not having the strength to cry out or having lost hope, knowing his end would soon come.

The squid's body tilted backward. Sections of its eight arms, looking like massive rubber hoses, floated to the surface. The feeding tentacle snaked toward the squid's parrot-like black bleak breaking above the ocean's surface. The obsidian mechanism pushed through white slimy muscle and opened wide. The beak looked strong enough to snap one of the *Sutton's* guns in half with a single bite.

Pratt entered the gaping maw feet first. Halfway in, the beak closed scissor-like, severing the unfortunate man above the waist. Face down, his arms slapped at the ocean's surface in a hopeless attempt to escape. Suffering was short-lived as the beak opened again. The rest of the sailor disappeared into the solid black cage, never to emerge again.

The feeding tentacle pulled away empty. The squid up-righted itself, seeming satisfied with its prize, and reached the tentacle up toward the deck for more.

The crewmen backed away, never taking their eyes from the impending danger.

Before anyone ran for their lives, an explosion reverberated from underneath. The enemy had drawn first blood.

The second explosion had Cummings thinking the war was already lost. Before he had time to grieve, a bright flash blanked his vision, and a thunderhead clapped against both ears.

CHAPTER 4

Lt. Bach peered through the attack periscope and updated coordinates to the helmsman and weapons officer.

Christoph stood with his eyes closed and back stiff. His mind's eye mapped out the battle scene before it happened. The U-boat would target the Destroyer with two G7e torpedoes and deliver the first strike. The torpedoes would speed to their destiny as stealthily and smoothly as any other marine life carved from billions of years of evolution. If the Americans did have time to react with an attack of their own, the deep waters of the Atlantic would allow him to hide in wait. Patience, knowing the enemy, thinking like the enemy, who was trained to engage him *as he thought*. Christoph knew how the game was played. He was not a commander to be stereotyped. Give the enemy what he's looking for, and then turn his folly into his destruction. He had made nineteen patrols in the war, and hundreds of thousands of tonnes of merchant vessels and their cargo had become sanctuaries for ocean dwellers by his hand. British and US war machines had succumbed to his wits, too. How many mariners did he send to rest with Davy Jones and his lot? Christoph didn't know, and he tried never to think of it. His orders were simply to find and sink his target, not take the lives of others. One wouldn't happen without the other, but again, it's a fact he didn't dwell on.

"In range and position," Bach said in a crisp, affirmative tone.

"Firing torpedoes," the weapon's officer said.

Christoph opened his eyes and looked over at Bach. The lieutenant gripped the periscope's handles, his body rigid as a rock. Seconds became hours in situations like these. It was as if the human spirit had some influence on future events. The wishing, the desire; unconsciously pleading for success to God, the Devil, the universe…it didn't matter. Victory the only objective, and at any cost.

"Torpedoes launched," the weapon's officer said.

"Godspeed," Christoph said, confidence in his voice.

Silence in the command room became palpable.

Faulk looked up from his sonar screen. "Commander, unknown approaching directly aft."

Slapped from his concentration, Christoph turned, narrowing eyes, and asked, "How far?"

"Nearly on top of us," Faulk said.

"How is that—?" Christoph's words stopped cold as small pops and shattering glass belched from the sonar station. The lights dimmed and pulsed, and the sub's battery-powered engines struggled.

The radar and sonar screens both went immediately dead. Faulk looked up with his eyes wide and a drooping lower chin. "The storm, it's over us. It engulfed the screen, blocking the radar out just before we lost it. It's affecting our electrical system."

Not forgetting the unknown streaking toward them, Christoph said, "Prepare to dive, then dive."

Bach was still behind the attack periscope. Christoph bee-lined over and pushed him aside. He turned 180° and lowered the periscope. The sub was still close enough to the surface to allow enough light for him to see a large creature coming toward them. It wasn't swimming noticeably fast, and he wondered how something this large, most likely a whale, had approached that close before being detected by the sonar.

"Controls aren't responding, sir. We cannot flood the ballasts," the helmsman said.

Christoph tore his gaze from the periscope's eye shield, and said, "Have the men do it manually." The sea creature's image remained in his mind. Something about it struck him as odd. A creature that size could only be a whale. Yet, while what his mind told him was logical, his eyes had told him something different.

"Radio is inoperable, sir," the helmsman said.

"Battery power is diminishing quickly. I do not know what is draining it so fast," Faulk said in a panicked tone.

"Get orders to the engine room. We need to dive!" Christoph said.

"Without batteries, we will not be able to pump out the ballast tanks and surface. Plus, we need power to generate oxygen." Bach stopped short of canceling the commander's order.

The lieutenant was right. Christoph had lost his cool and made decisions without thinking everything through. Maybe the stress of a U-boat commander *was* finally taking its toll. "Take us high enough for the snorkel to catch air. Start the diesel engines and continue on the previous course to South America. If we cannot see the Americans in the storm, then they cannot see us, either."

He quickly returned his gaze back through the periscope. The creature was closer and much clearer, and what he saw, he could barely believe.

The behemoth was not a whale.

It was a shark, identified by its blunt snout and rows of sharp teeth. A shark half as tall as *U-616* and a third of its length! How could such a monster exist?

The megalodon eased past the U-boat like a creeping locomotive. Christoph watched in fascination at the meter-long teeth jutting from a mouth wide enough to swallow ten men whole. The vacant black eyes reminded him of a sailor's stare into the unknown horizon after death. The gills opened and closed in constant rhythm as the tail propelled it smoothly through the ocean and past the *U-616*.

Christoph had seen many sharks in his life. A sailor fears only the cold more than the ocean-faring predator if he found himself forced to abandon ship. One thing for sure, something this large would have little chance sneaking up on them, which didn't explain why the sonar didn't ping it sooner. Right before the storm overtook them, it was as if the giant shark was placed in the water right next to them.

The diesel engines rolled lazily over, and the command room lights dimmed further. Either the batteries were too low to get them started or else something in the mysterious storm had affected their electronics.

"It is no good, sir," the helmsman said.

"Crap," Christoph said and stepped away from the periscope.

"You saw nothing outside?" Bach asked.

"Nothing to be concerned about. We have greater problems than marine life. It was a shark. A very big shark—as large as a whale. It moved past us, probably looking for deeper waters to feed."

"Orders, Commander?" Bach asked, a loyal sailor waiting to do the bidding of his captain.

It always came down to the decision of one man. One man deciding the fate of fifty-two passengers in an underwater boat blinded by a storm, and losing power by the second.

A thud and a groan of hollow metal told them the *U-616* had bumped into something. The boat listed a few degrees to one side.

Christoph and Bach locked gazes for a brief moment, and then the commander raced over to the periscope.

The massive shark had returned and was directly forward. Damn the luck! Christoph imagined that the sputtering diesel engines had drawn its attention, and its primordial curiosity had it checking out the potential prey the only way it knew how: *with its teeth.*

A SK C/35 naval gun mounted on the forward deck acted like a fishing lure. The megalodon had bumped it with its snout, and still not certain if it was food or not, bit down on it.

Metal creaked, and the sub, though barely moving in the water, slowed enough for the sailors in the command room to check their balance.

"That damn shark is back. It is attacking the gun," Christoph said.

"A shark?" the helmsman said.

"I told you it was big," Christoph said.

The sub listed further, sliding the crew sideways. Options at this point were few to none. Christoph ordered, "To the surface, now! Use the last of the compressed air to empty the ballast. We've got to shake this thing."

A crewman waiting in the corner made an immediate exit to execute the order.

It was a shame the gun wasn't remotely operated. The 8.8cm shells fired into the belly of the beast, despite its size, would surely be the end of it. But it took a crew of three men to load and fire the weapon once on the surface. If they couldn't shoot the shark, at least they could present less of a target to entice it.

The U-boat slowly lifted, but it listed so much now that everyone slid toward the wall. The rear of the sub started floating upward, leaving the front end struggling past the weight of the megalodon. A bad situation had just gotten worse.

Metal groaned again. What fascination did this shark have with steel? It couldn't eat it. Then Christoph realized why. Anger. The shark saw the U-boat as a threat to its territory.

The rear of the boat finally stopped rising. It had found the surface. Abruptly, the front end sprang up as the weight of the megalodon no longer held it in check. It had given up the battle, at least for now.

As the U-boat stabilized, Christoph adjusted his trousers and straightened his collar. "You are in charge, Bach. I'm taking a look outside."

*

Erik Neuzetser had remained in the narrow hall just outside of the sickbay. When the boat tilted, he laid on the floor and held on for safety. He had no idea what was going on with the US Destroyer but was confident that his father would save them. Erik trusted his father without question. His father loved him, shown by his actions if not by his words. Still, the man saw life through his own experiences, his own beliefs. Erik wasn't his father. He was his own person, an individual. Did he have the fortitude to declare to his father that *he was his own man*?

Despite his father's vast knowledge and success, he just didn't understand.

Erik had been raised to be a man who could care for himself. That was fine, but when his views of life veered from what his father thought best, he lost favor. That wasn't fair. A free thinker had to be allowed to think without limit, not confined to borders within a certain philosophy.

He was a loyal German; no one could have said otherwise. But in Youth Camp, he had many questions that he could only ask his father. Moral questions, basic right and wrong. Yes, the Aryans were the superior race. But some of the rumors he overheard had him concerned. Even if the Jews were a blight to mankind, they were at least as valuable as animals. He had never heard of animals treated as badly as the rumors of what was done to the Jews.

His father never directly answered his concerns. Instead, he advised him to follow the Führer's plan and *would understand when he was older*. Understanding can come at any age, and Erik felt like he was capable now. Camp had taught him many things, including how to fight the enemies. If he was trusted to go to war and give his life, then nothing should have been held back from him.

"It appears we have surfaced," Adolf Eichmann said. The tallish man, dressed in a black suit, stood next to two cots. His face was thin and long, with a nose a bit too large, and bat-like ears on the sides of his head. The former Nazi SS lieutenant colonel had helped others in the room stabilize the cots when the boat rose unevenly to the surface.

The two patients, a man, and a woman sat up on their cots and looked around.

The man was bald, but it looked to Erik like his head had been recently shaved because there was some fine stubble returning. His face and neck, just like the woman's, was heavily bandaged. The eyes, nose, and mouth were uncovered enough to function. A result of Allied bombing, or so he was told. His hands continually trembled.

The woman's hair was an unnatural shade of black, obviously colored. Her gaze darted back and forth across the room. Erik wondered if pain medication had her incoherent.

Erik had learned the patients were Frank Viktor and his wife, Gisela. But at no time did anyone is sickbay call them by their names. This struck Erik as odd, for some reason.

"We will not surrender if we are captured," Dr. Josef Mengele said, his eyes dark and sunk into the back of his head. He opened a cabinet and pushed some small containers to the side, retrieving a cobalt blue glass pill bottle. "Cyanide."

"I have looked death in the eye many of times. I am not afraid," Franz Stangl said. "I only wish I had my zither to play one last song."

"I never figured you for the sentimental type, Franz," Klaus Barbie said. "Tell me, did you play for any of your guests in the euthanasia camps?"

Stangl's upper lip rose toward his nose, and with half-closed eyes, he said, "They would not have appreciated my efforts. The zither brings me peace. I learned to play to block the memories of my father."

The male patient reached down the side of the cot and patted the head of a German Shepherd.

Erik had no clue of where Frank Viktor fit in the SS rankings. He knew the other men in the room had high credentials, and they catered to Viktor. Bringing a dog from Germany all the way to South America seemed ridiculous. Who amongst the elite would afford such privilege?

The Leader had a dog, it occurred to Erik, a German Shepherd. But the Leader was dead.

Who was the man underneath the bandages? Who was the woman? One had a shaved head and the other dyed hair. Yes, the man's injury may have necessitated shaving of the head, but nothing associated with woman's injuries mandated the coloring of the hair.

They had a German Shepherd.

Was it possible…?

"Good dog, Brandi…good dog," the man in the cot said, and sighed deeply.

*

The U-boat's conning tower hatch opened. Christoph looked into an ethereal sky of green clouds and fog hovering above the ocean. This storm didn't seem to bring any rain with it. Because of how it had interfered with both radar and sonar, he wondered if the storm was *electrical* in nature. Was that even possible? None of his military briefings had ever warned of such.

The fog thinned rapidly. Christoph brought up his binoculars and looked forward. After scanning several seconds, he saw part of a huge dorsal fin heading out to sea. Good, the giant shark had lost interest in his steel fish.

A bright flash as invasive as someone shining a searchlight in his face in a pitch-dark room had his hands up to his eyes. Thunder cracked as if directly behind him. Christoph lowered himself a few steps down the ladder, wondering what had just happened.

The U-boat violently jolted, he almost slipped off the ladder as the world tilted sideways. This impact was nothing like what the shark had delivered. This felt like they hit something solid, maybe immoveable.

Things felt dead still. The slight ring in his ears from the thunder diminished. Christoph climbed the uncomfortable angle a few feet and looked about again.

There was a good reason why the U-boat felt motionless. *U-616* rested atop a sandy beach. The ocean waves rolled and licked its hull.

CHAPTER 5

It took several seconds for Brazo's head to clear after the shock of the flash and loud thunder. He was a bit surprised to see the command room intact and everyone more or less still at their stations. *Alive*, at their stations. He initially felt the last event had been a direct hit with an aerial bomb from a plane. That hadn't happened. He wasn't sure what caused the commotion, and he didn't have time to play twenty questions.

"I'm going on deck," Brazo said; there was no need for explanations. "You." He pointed to one of the crewmen waiting for orders. "Follow me."

"Yes, sir," the crewman said, quickly following behind the captain as he fast stepped to the next compartment and up a ladder.

The *Sutton* had been hit. Two times for sure by torpedoes, and this wasn't the first time Brazo had been in this situation. The question was, *how bad was the damage*? He had been an officer on the *USS Kearny* back in 1941 when it took a torpedo from a U-boat while patrolling off the coast of Greenland. Destroyers had their share of armor and other safety features, but nothing like battleships, cruisers, or aircraft carriers. Ships of those classes had heavy armor, anti-torpedo belts, watertight compartments, and elaborate damage control systems. Destroyers were commonly referred to as *tin cans*. Still, the *Kearny*, hit starboard in the forward fire room, avoided flooding by a fast-acting crew, and managed to escape safely.

Brazo exited to the deck under the pilot room. Black smoke rolled from one of the engine rooms near the middle of the ship, next to the fuel tank. An oily sheen spread across the surface of the water.

As bad as it looked, it only became worse when he saw smoke coming from the rear of the ship, right where ammunition was stored for the big guns. That's a fire that couldn't be quenched. The fire wouldn't stop until every ounce of propellant went up in smoke.

His gaze drifted over to where he expected to see ocean kissing the horizon and got the biggest shock of all.

Land.

There was land not a half mile from the ship. Land with mighty trees and thick foliage growing past a sandy beach. Land with high hills and rocky formations. It was a virtual paradise. Land that shouldn't be there, but none of that mattered. His ship didn't have long before it would find the ocean's bottom. There was no sense in wasting men's lives trying to save an unwinnable battle. Brazo turned to the crewman, and said, "Pass out my order, abandon ship, abandon ship!"

The crewman disappeared down the ladder, excitingly hollering the captain's order as he made his way back to the command center.

There was a megaphone in the pilot room above. Brazo grabbed the ladder leading up and headed for it.

*

The giant squid's feeding tentacle unfolded as it rose toward the ship's deck. Its suction cups bluish-white on the edges, quivering for a hold on its next victim. The ghastly one eye hovered from above, seeing all just like a God. The world was for its taking. It was hungry and would feed well this day.

Cummings and the other three realized the hunt began anew. The four turned and scattered, but one crewman had taken only two steps when he twisted his ankle and stumbled to his knees. The feeding tentacle scooped him up and dragged him across the deck, leaving a thin trail of slime. "No! No! Noooo...." His cry faded into the wind, echoing across the abyss of time to reside with the death cries of mariners before him.

Thick, black smoke billowed from the engine room. Cummings knew if the fire team didn't get things under control in a hurry, then he had the choice of riding the *Sutton* to the bottom of the ocean or facing final judgment in the squid's horrific beak. He had heard drowning was one of the better ways to die, although the thought of starving for air terrified him. But it wasn't supposed to be like *holding your breath*, with your lungs crying out for oxygen. It was said, once you breached the fear of breathing underwater, the lungs quickly filled, and with that, death overtook you like a consuming sleep after working in the field for a long day.

"This is Captain Brazo. Abandon ship! Abandon ship!" Brazo's voice sounded tinny as it belted from the megaphone. The train of smoke chugging from the fuel tank masked his location.

It was then Cummings turned his attention starboard beam and saw land. Land! They weren't anywhere near land before. At first he thought it was just a small island, but as he turned his gaze from side to side, the land stretched as far as the eye could see.

Sailors' cries and screams rose as more advanced from the burning hulk and arrived on deck. Both of the giant squid's feeding tentacles were up and busy gathering food for its belly.

The captain's orders to abandon ship continued. Cummings heard the hiss of the compressed gas cylinders inflating as the life rafts hit the water. The crew was bailing opposite side of the giant squid. With the *Sutton* between them, it might buy enough time for the survivors to reach land. But there was no guarantee. The squid could dive beneath the ship, sensing them in the water. When it emerged on the other side, its massive weight could upset the life rafts and spill his mates into the deep.

Smoke rose from mid and aft of the ship. Sailors emerging onto the deck scattered like insects. None suspected the horror of the sea god as its tentacles delivered their deadly wrath.

Cummings was no hero and never pretended to be, not to others, and certainly not himself. Something inside grabbed his fear and quickly killed it. With his resolve hardened, his gaze turned to the 20mm anti-aircraft gun a short hike up nearby stairs.

With land so close by, he and the others stood a chance of making it off the ship safely. But not with this monster set to spoil the lives of others only to fill a gut that would be empty again the next day.

The aircraft gun sat five feet high and operated on a swivel. He quickly positioned the barrel toward the giant squid.

Another of his shipmates left the safe harbor of the deck, a feeding tentacle wrapped tightly around him. The sailor's cry for help all but lost over the pandemonium and the captain barking orders over the megaphone.

He placed his body between the gun's shoulder rest and cranked the elevation handle until sighting the squid between the shield.

There it was, that huge round eye trying again to steal his soul. Not this time. The squid would learn what it's like to take on the US Navy. The 20mm shells could take a plane out of the sky. The squid was massive but still made of flesh. Cummings didn't know where its brain resided to go in for a quick kill. Poking it in the eye and blinding it seemed like a good place to start.

He aimed, leaning into the shoulder rest, and squeezed the trigger.

20mm missiles ripped from the gun's barrel straight toward the monster's eye. A sailor trapped in a feeding tentacle flew through the air, only to crash on deck and land in a crumpled heap as the slimy appendage flung haphazardly about. An angry, hollow hiss of air bellowed out, mixed with gulps and gurgles of sea water.

The squid moved quickly, the eye no longer in his sights. The mantle provided a large target, and if the brain did hide somewhere in there, Cummings wanted to find it. Round after round pelted the nasty beast.

Tentacles crashed up and down on the deck. The squid might not be able to see, but it did stay to fight. Cummings cringed as one of the appendages swiped right above his head. *That was close, too close*, he thought. Didn't matter, he would stay until every last shell had left the gun and it clicked empty.

The eerie hiss of air burped from the squid once more, sounding more like a whimper this time.

"That's what you get for messin' with the US Navy!" Cummings shouted among the gun's rattle.

The squid's mantle sank fast into the ocean, its feeding tentacles pulled from the deck and slithered back with it. The water turned jet black where it had been. A wake traced its path as it fled for the safety of the deep.

He did it! Ralph Cummings had won. He was a hero and he had earned it.

Fast stepping down the stairs and to the deck, he raised a fist and laughed.

The captain continued to give orders over the megaphone. The ship set noticeably lower in the water. More sailors bailed off the other side. It was time for him to leave, too.

Cummings took a deep breath of air, strangely mixed with the sea, squid funk, and burning petroleum. He took a few steps forward when something wet and slimy closed around him. His head reeled as he was lifted into the air and pulled backward. He was in the deadly grasp of a feeding tentacle. But how?

The ocean boiled underneath, and the drill bit-shaped stabilizing fin of a giant squid breached the surface. The massive mantle followed, and then the eye rose until it was dead even with him. The black orb stared back from a glob of clear gelatin.

The strength Cummins once had melted. A slow stream of urine trickled down his leg. The suctions cups drew tightly against his skin to the point he thought it would tear. He had wrongly assumed there was only one giant squid. His first battle had been for naught. He had failed his shipmates.

The squid's curiosity didn't last long. Cummings watched the sky pull away as the tentacle lowered toward the surface. The sharp beak, its pointy tips protruding from the sickening white membrane, opened wide for its first taste of human.

Cummings so now wished he had the opportunity to drown.

The beak came down, severing him in half. Just like Pratt, he found his arms fighting to paddle to safety. Just like Pratt, the second bite sent him to the belly of the beast.

*

Time was the enemy. The *Sutton* didn't have long before she swallowed too much ocean and sunk. Still, it pleased Brazo to see numerous life rafts bobbing in the water and sailors quickly reaching safety. There were nearly three hundred men aboard the ship. The torpedoes from the U-boat undoubtedly had killed a number of men. The torpedo that hit the *Kearny* had snuffed out twenty-two lives. There was no way to know how many men had perished after the two torpedoes hit the *Sutton.*

He counted over twenty life rafts in the water and heard the splashes of more going off the side of the ship, each boat capable of seating fifteen sailors. Crews quickly loaded emergency supplies and weapons from the armory to the waiting rafts below. His men responded to the emergency like a well-oiled machine, despite the utter chaos of the situation. Sure, he had run the *abandon ship* simulation many times before. In real life, though, there was no way to know how the crew would respond. He couldn't simulate a raging fire pumping smoke into parts of the ship. Nor the unnerving knowledge that some of their buddies had been pulverized and barbecued minutes before. Human nature programmed men to panic. The most important thing in an emergency was staying calm and rational. Despite all the screams and cries, the action of his crew proved they had received their training well.

Brazo had been so caught up in his overseeing that the bark of a 20mm gun had gone on for several seconds before it dawned on him. They weren't being attacked by aircraft, were they? He quickly looked over in the direction of the gunshots, and then to the sky. The smoke walled off his view, preventing him from seeing what was going on that part of the ship. The sky, what he could see of it, was clear of aircraft. Who was firing the gun? Why? Maybe someone had lost their cool. Had the U-boat surfaced? Was it about to attack again?

Brazo left the pilot room to see for himself. The water was dangerously close to reaching the deck. There would be no time for him to do that now, and the gun had gone silent too.

He looked around and saw the last of his men climbing into the waiting life rafts. *Is this everyone?* he asked himself. An inner urge compelled him to search the ship one last time to be sure. That would be certain death, as time left him two options: go down with the ship or live to fight another day. He broke his reverie after a barrage of calls from XO Slick.

"Captain! Captain! Captain! We need to leave now," Slick yelled.

"Is this it? Are any men left aboard?" Brazo asked.

"I believe all survivors are off, sir."

Brazo looked deep into Slick's eyes and believed the man was telling the truth. The weight of others' lives was a heavy burden who only the pure realized. Three short steps down the rope ladder had him in the life raft with ten crewmen.

The paddles came out and dipped into the water. The captain and his crew bobbed on the ocean in a flotilla of yellow life rafts.

Brazo did a quick count and a crude estimation; fifty or sixty of his men didn't make it. It could have been more, but he seriously doubted it was less. His heart sank, and his mind flashed with the faces of all the brave men who stepped on the *Sutton's* deck for its shakedown. Who of them had made the *Sutton* their sepulcher? Then, his mind saw pretty wives crying, clinging to their children, learning that their beloveds would never return home.

Letting out one huff of bad air, Brazo cleared his mind. He was the captain. The men who survived were in his command. His duty was to get them to safety, and from there, figure out a way to get back home.

CHAPTER 6

With the batteries dead and the U-boat listing at an angle, Christoph had given the order to exit and make camp on land. All fifty-two of his crew and passengers were safe. There was at least that consolation. Where they were, and the next move, was unknown. Their planned destination had contacts waiting for them with new papers, new identities, and locations where they could start over in life. Christoph looked forward to that. It was a bitter thing to lose the war, but now at least he had a chance to become closer to Erik. He would be there to guide him in his ascent into manhood, just as his father had done for him. It would take time, but time he would have. Christoph planned to buy a boat and catch fish for his new life's work. Erik would be his first mate. They would have plenty of time to rub the rough edges of their relationship together until it became a smooth fit. All of that would have to wait. He was the commander, and other issues took precedent.

Several kilometers to the southeast, past a dense forest that hid anything from view, black smoke formed an ashen gray cloud against a clear blue sky. There was no doubt this was a petrol fire. He'd seen it too often in the last serval years. The *U-616*'s torpedoes had found their mark, hitting the Destroyer. This complicated the situation further. There would be survivors aboard the ship. A Destroyer's complement of sailors greatly outnumbered the occupants of a smaller U-boat.

His crew was at least well-equipped with arms and ammunition. Continuing the war was certainly something he hadn't planned on. At least, it seemed to him, he had the advantage of the element of surprise. The Americans *might* suspect the *U-616* to be in the area. Certainly not on dry land, and surely with no idea of location. Should he lead a raid against the Americans and use surprise to defeat them? It was an option. An option his heart didn't want to follow, but he knew his head would ultimately decide.

A murmur arose from behind him, just where the sandy beach ended and hard ground and grass began. He turned and saw a crewman pointing to the sky. Others shielded their eyes against the sun and looked too. The murmur rose.

Christoph lifted his gaze to see what caused the commotion. A bird of some sort, perhaps a frigate bird, circled overhead. As it moved out of the sun's glare, he realized it wasn't a bird at all.

The creature was bat-like in a way and reminded him of a dragon from one of Erik's children's books. Its upperparts were tannish-green in color and underside the same, only streaked with white. The head had a triangular shape at the top, and its bill was long and flat.

SKEER-AK!

A shiver ran down Christoph's spine as the beast's cry cut deeply into his rationale. His schooling had included the study of fossils in one of his science classes. He remembered a flying reptile named *pterodactyl*, a pterosaur, from the time when dinosaurs roamed the Earth. From the skeletal remains and drawings, this creature could be nothing other than that. But that was impossible. Dinosaurs had been extinct for millions of years.

He scanned the nearest trees and listened intently over the growing surprise of the crew. There weren't any birds nearby. *Strange*. Could this be an island evolution had ignored? This was 1945, every corner of the Earth had been explored by this point, and nothing like this had ever been found.

The storm. The storm had something to do with them being there. It certainly had moved them through space and set them on land. How, he didn't know. But, did the storm do more than that? Did the storm move them back in time?

Impossible. Time travel only existed in fiction. If it were possible to manipulate time, then Hitler would have had his best scientists working to perfect it.

"Commander," Lt. Bach said. He had stepped over while Christoph had been lost in his thoughts. "What do you think *that* is?"

"Probably the same thing as you. It's a prehistoric creature, a pterodactyl."

"There have not been any prehistoric creatures alive since the prehistory of man."

"Well, I would say you are wrong at this point. There is at least one."

Bach went to speak, but Christoph raised his hand.

"I can't explain our situation at this point. This is what we know: We are on an unknown island that has a large flying reptile. I seriously doubt it is alone, so we need to keep our wits about in case it decides to risk a chance at tasting humans. What other kinds of life might we encounter, we do not know. But," he said as he pointed southeast, "look at the smoke. We do know the Destroyer that found us is several kilometers away. We must first make a temporary camp and decide our moves. I will send out recon missions to get a lay of the land. Hopefully, we will find a semblance of civilization and a means off this island, and soon be on our way back to South America."

***

Camp was set a short distance inland. Trudging through the dense jungle had been an arduous task. Each crewman carried a personal shoulder pack with minimum provisions. And all had to carry rations and weapons that had been stored aboard the boat.

Christoph decided, along with the other representatives of the SS, to take refuge just west at a rocky embankment several stories high. The solid wall provided defense on one side, and to their fortune, provided cavernous holes large enough to offer a semblance of shelter for the entire company. Accommodations were almost as comfortable as the U-boat, and passages leading to the open sky were only a few steps away. Bedrolls had to be rationed, as bunks on the U-boat only bedded half the men at a time. U-boats were only large enough to allow half the crew to walk about. So, the other half had to stay in bunks out of the way.

"White Eagle to Troster One, over," Otto Faulk said, the back of his hand glistening with sweat. He had been at his duty for nearly a half hour. "White Eagle to Troster One, over."

"Perhaps the granite hill behind us is blocking the radio signal," Eichmann said. His tone had been even, but his words always seemed to carry a veiled threat.

"We tried the radio at the beach before following the group here," Bach said. "The results were the same."

Faulk grabbed the hand crank on the radio and turned it several times. "White Eagle to Troster One, over."

"Perhaps the radio is broken, no?" Barbie said. "You reported the ship's communications had malfunctioned during the storm."

"We considered that and opened the radio. There were broken tubes. Any tubes connected to electrical equipment shattered during the storm. The spare tubes in boxes were intact. We replaced the tubes, and there is no reason for the radio not to work."

"The radio *is* working," Faulk said as he methodically changed bands.

"What do you mean?" Eichmann asked.

"The static. I know the radio is working because of the atmospheric noise. What I do not understand is why I cannot pick up any other transmissions. There is always chatter somewhere on the radio band. Radio waves can travel hundreds, even thousands of miles depending on signal strength and atmospheric conditions. I have never seen a time when the airwaves were totally silent," Faulk said.

"Interesting," Eichmann said. He cocked his head to the side and stared off into infinity, not bothering to share his thoughts.

Christoph had mentally given up on the radio almost from the start. There was plenty of evidence to suggest he and his crew were no longer in 1945. Evidence he fought to accept. After seeing the pterodactyl, he remembered that giant sharks roamed the ocean in prehistoric times. Two creatures existing outside his normal timeline was more than just an oddity. It strengthened the idea that their existence was the norm, and he and his crew were the ones severely out of place. But in reality, there were more than just two strange creatures. On the trip to the rocky shelter, many small creatures skittered away through the foliage. They were fast and their skin colored to camouflage them well in the lush environment. Of those few he caught a glimpse of, he couldn't identify specifically. They were at least reptilian or perhaps even amphibian, seeing as they were so close to the sea. But he could have sworn he saw them running on *two legs* instead of four. It was hard to tell, as the creatures were low to the ground. And as far as birds, he did see a few nearby. Unfortunately, he didn't have time to put on his glasses before they flew away. These birds had feathers but were noticeably different from European birds. Of the three he saw, their legs were larger, and their bodies and heads actually appeared reptile-like. Their flight of escape was without the grace of a modern bird, nor had they sung sweet tunes, sounding only in strange pops and rasps.

"You can stop now," Christoph said to Faulk.

Relief loosened the tight expression on Faulk's face. "Yes, sir." He quickly secured the microphone, picked up the radio, and headed toward one of the caves used as material storage.

Dr. Mengele stepped from the cave offering refuge to the two patients, Frank and Gisela Viktor. The man carried himself in a slow and determined gait, which drew all eyes upon him by the time he arrived. "I take it our situation has failed to progress any further."

"We are secure for the moment. Beyond that, we will take any opportunity presented to us to get us closer to our objective," Christoph said and wondered how long the esteemed members of the SS on this journey would continue the charade of civility. Eichmann, Barbie, Stangl, and Mengele were men of strong wills, each demanding perfection in their own commands. Who would rise among them first to challenge his command? And what of Frank Viktor? Christoph found it strange that he had never heard of the man before he arrived on *U-616*. He was told Viktor was a civilian and a secret confidant to the Führer himself. One thing was for certain, the four SS officers acted subservient to the man, and to a lesser extent, his wife, *as if he were the Führer himself.*

Then the realization hit him. He had been so focused on the mission and his son Erik that the possibility never occurred to him that *Frank and Gisela Viktor* might possibly be *Adolph Hitler and*

Eva Braun. Rochus Misch had been witness to the Führer's and his wife's suicides. Misch's report, that both took cyanide capsules, and Hitler had put a gun to his own head and pulled the trigger, eliminated any future thought that the Führer had somehow escaped.

"The patients, are they still in good spirits?" Christoph asked.

"Yes, surprisingly so," Mengele said. "Their injuries are healing nicely and," he stopped to take a deep breath, "both tell me the air on this land has refreshed them."

"Just being outdoors is enough to revive anyone's spirit," Bach said. "Especially someone who is not used to spending days cooped up inside a U-boat, breathing recycled air expelled from fifty other men."

"No, it is something more than that," Mengele said. "The air is, so to say, heavier, richer, and *not* with humidity."

Once again Christoph's mind returned to his science class. The prehistoric world's oxygen level in the atmosphere was just over 30%, significantly more than the 21% of his modern world. The theory went that some life in prehistoric times was able to grow to gargantuan size because of the increased oxygen. This would explain why he didn't get winded on his trip through the jungle to here.

By this time, Franz Stangl had joined the gathering. He looked impatient, roaming his gaze and not fixating on a point for more than a split-second. "What is next, Commander? I wanted to buy a ticket for the next train out, but I could not find a station."

Well, at least someone found humor in the situation. "I have sent out two recon groups of five men each. They will map an area a few kilometers wide north and southeast of our position. Their orders are to return by noon tomorrow. We will know more by then."

"The trains always ran on time under the Führer's watch," Eichmann wistfully said.

The lieutenant colonel's words brought an ache to Christoph's gut, robbed of the glorious hope once felt of what the Fatherland had achieved, and the future that had been lost.

Several meters away, Erik worked dutifully with two other crewmen wiping down the rifles and checking loads of ammunition.

Christoph felt an uncontrollable urge to hug his son and headed off to see him.

CHAPTER 7

Brazo's heart sank along with the *USS Sutton*. He hadn't had time to form an emotional bond with the ship, though, having only been in command for a few weeks. The two shared no battle scars or memories. It's just that the ship was such a magnificent creation: sixteen hundred tons of battle steel hardened by human sweat, capable of unimaginable destruction. Thousands of man-hours toiled in its birth, but in a matter of minutes, a death blow had sent it to the bottom of the ocean to sleep forever. Such a waste on so many levels. Its demise exacerbated exponentially by the poor souls who went down with it.

The aft was the last part of the ship consumed by the ocean's mouth. It stuck spear-like at an angle and slowly disappeared. The ship's mass pulled in a shallow spinning vortex, threatening to take those near with it. Fortunately, the life rafts were far enough away, escaping one disastrous fate for an unknown other.

Oil mixed with the greenish water and small waves caressed the surface. The ship was gone as if it had never been there; its stories, its memories, its future, gone with it.

Damn the war! Damn every threat to freedom. Man had progressed so far above the animals, and to his shame, some of his greatest achievements weren't designed to save lives, but to take them.

Brazo forced the poisons weighing down his soul from his mind. He couldn't dwell on what was lost. His job was to preserve what he still had.

The twenty-something life rafts spread a large swath of ocean, all heading for the shore.

He turned his gaze to the men in his raft. XO Slick had been staring at him and quickly looked out toward land. Undoubtedly, he had been gauging Brazo's reaction. Was he expecting the captain to break down over losing his ship? Or was this a learning moment for him? If Brazo could maintain his composure, then the XO would know that would be expected of him. Men followed the examples of their leaders. Having the confidence and respect of your crew alone could determine the outcome of the battle. Today, Brazo would give his crew no reason to lose heart.

Jim Stone paddled dutifully with the other crewmen. Jim was a humble man of great character. His devotion to God and His Son unquestionable. He had an uncanny knowledge of electronics, and there wasn't anything electrical he couldn't troubleshoot. As nice of a man as he was, those who tried to push someone of his diminutive stature around soon learned they had a virtual tiger by the tail. Jim Stone was one scrappy fellow once prodded over the edge. Brazo thought it was a good thing Stone didn't care for strong drink, as he would have made one mean drunk.

The others in the boat were regular crewmen; variously ranked, and most under the age of thirty. One of them, Adam Rodrigue, looked too young to shave. Another, Danny Underwood, didn't look that much older. He knew some seventeen-year-olds had legally joined the Navy, and often wondered if any sixteen-year-olds had slipped in.

Something from his left peripheral caught his eye. The ocean bubbled not far from a raft several yards over. *Sharks*? He hoped not. The last thing they needed now was a school of sharks coming by to take a mouthful of the raft, or worse.

Then he thought he saw something float to the surface of the water. It was reddish, reminding him of a hot dog in color. The end of the object lifted out of the water and raised up over the raft. At first, he didn't know what to make of it, thinking something from the Sutton had floated to the surface. But the object unfolded and spread wide. Massive whitish suction cups with blue edges, looking like beach balls cut in half, threatened the raft's occupants.

The moment was surreal, challenging Brazo on an unexplored level. His mind struggled at what he saw and what it meant.

A sailor yelled as he looked up at the feeding tentacle looming above. The suction cups pulsed with life, seemingly like mouths opening and closing.

A raft mate abandoned his paddle and grabbed at his hip, coming away with a service pistol. He began firing before aiming, but a wasted bullet or two was insignificant. He unloaded the magazine as the appendage came down, capturing three of the men in the rubber raft.

Four sailors had been lucky enough to spill out the side into the ocean. They swam away as fast as they could.

"My God, what is that?" Brazo said, helpless to do anything but watch.

Slick pulled up his sidearm and held it at the ready.

Some fifty feet away from the captured raft, something mountainous pushed up past the surface. A drill bit-shaped stabilizing fin larger than five bull elephants standing nose to tail emerged and continued skyward until a ghastly all-seeing eye of monstrous proportions entered the light of day.

"Kraken." Brazo had spoken the mythical creature's name in a whisper. His subconscious had assigned the name to something that only existed in legend.

Growing up, he had read many ocean tales. The kraken was lord of the sea and showed interlopers no mercy in their folly to travel the waters of his kingdom. The mighty beast would swim underneath unsuspecting vessels, giving no thought of the tiny creatures who crawled on top. Its eight arms would slither up the hull and snake along the deck until finding a bowsprit, the mizzen, the main mast, or the foremast and take hold. The tiny creatures aboard would yell, scream, and fire their puny weapons. Their efforts would be for naught.

The kraken did not take revenge in haste. It savored the spoils of its victory one victim at a time. As more of its arms weighed down the ship, the two feeding tentacles searched and caught what would prove to be a tasty meal. No man could stop the powerful crush of its beak. In the end, the captain of the ship proved to be as ordinary as the lowest deck mate. The kraken would rise above the wooden vessel and relegate its fate to the bottom of the ocean. The arrogance of man invading the kraken's lair came at a price. The price was always the same: *total destruction.*

The first sailor to enter the giant squid's beak cried out to God and begged for mercy. Salvation was not at hand, but perhaps mercy was. The sailor's plea was snuffed out in mid-sentence. Hopefully, the end had come quickly.

XO Slick steadied his hand and fired two rounds toward the massive mantle. His Colt M1911 .45 had short range accuracy. Brazo thought there was little chance of the bullets even finding their target.

Random gunshots popped off from various life rafts. Sailors had unpacked M1 Garand rifles and attempted to give the men swimming for safety a fighting chance.

Stone had his M1 ready and steadied his aim with an elbow on the raft's edge before squeezing off rounds.

More death cries spoke the fate of the captured sailors. Each had been devoured by a creature a third of the size of the *Sutton.*

The sailors in the water, one by one, began to disappear as the feeding tentacles quickly harvested their precious flesh.

Guns had seemed to have no effect on the giant squid. Seven men had met an undeserved fate.

The captain has two choices when it comes to battle: *fight or flee.* If they were out in the middle of the ocean, then he would have had no choice but to group and fight the thing to the last man. But land was too close and the odds against them too obvious. It was again time to flee. The thought left a bitter taste in his mouth, but his head must always overrule his heart.

"Stop firing and make shore!" Brazo still had the megaphone with him, and, at this distance, everyone should have heard the order. "All men take up paddles and head to shore."

Slick shot a questioning gaze at Brazo.

"You too, XO," Brazo said.

Jim Stone didn't need affirmation. The man secured his rifle and picked up his paddle.

A large splash followed by screams of surprised meant the kraken was not yet satiated. Another raft full of men caught in the vile suckers, and a tentacle that ferried them, would see their last sunset.

Brazo gritted his teeth. A snarl pulled his upper lip toward his nose. With fire in his eyes, he yelled through the megaphone, "To the shore! To the shore! To the shore!"

His men had to stay focused. It was the only way any had a chance of surviving. Again, time was not in their favor. The quicker to dry ground, or at least to water depths unsuited for a giant squid, the better. "To the shore! To the shore! To the shore!"

He then realized the cadence of his order mimicked the drummer on a Viking ship. He was setting a pace for all to follow. He watched Stone and the others stroke in rhythm to his command. Looking around, it was evident the other rafts were, too.

More terror-filled cries, and then another raft disappeared into the deep.

How many more men had to die? Brazo looked up into the sky and had the urge to curse God, and would have if he only believed. Ironically, it almost seemed worthy to accept the unseen, just to have the satisfaction to blame this situation on someone else. Then it wouldn't be his responsibility. Someone else, a higher power, would excuse him.

Brazo pushed his weak thoughts from his mind. He was T.W. Brazo, and he would look anyone, including Death, in the eye and own the situation.

He continued his chant, but the megaphone's volume rapidly began to decrease. Weak battery. *Damn the luck*! Not now. Not this close.

Water rolled over something larger than a man toward them just beneath the surface, off the starboard bow. The slick dark green crown of the creature's head peaked first.

"Starboard bow!" Brazo yelled as he reached for his side weapon.

All eyes in the raft turned and saw a huge, relatively flat, elongated snake-like head periscope from the water. The sea creature opened its mouth, brandishing rows of railroad spike-like teeth. The six front top and bottom teeth slightly jutted forward, making it easier to skewer its prey. The head kept rising on a long neck that at first seemed endless. The neck rose well above ten feet from the water.

The occupants of the raft had certainly captured its curiosity. It patiently assessed the interloper and meandered its head about as if it were choosing which morsel to sample first. Then, its reptilian-like eyes bulged, eager for action.

They were backed into a corner. It was time to fight.

Brazo drew first blood as he aimed his pistol and fired at the head. The bullet smashed into the side of the creature's mouth. Bits of teeth and splatters of red blood erupted from the projectile's impact. The .45 caliber wasn't the fastest of bullets, only traveling 830 feet per second. Its more than half-ounce of lead carried a considerable impact at that speed, though.

The elasmosaurus hissed in obvious pain. Before it had a chance to retaliate, the beast became the target of four handguns and one rifle. Only a few bullets made contact as its head and neck swung wildly about. It was enough to take the fight out of it. The head went back underwater, and the elasmosaurus dove underneath the raft.

The pit in Brazo's stomach deepened. This beast was huge! The water clear enough for him to see the entire length of its body as it passed underneath the raft. He guessed it to be nearly fifty feet!

"They don't grow fish that big in Tennessee," Stone said, his M1 at the ready in case the thing decided to turn around and try again.

"We need to get to shore," Brazo said. He kept his vigil with gun firmly gripped in both hands by his side.

The crew quickly manned their positions and began paddling again. At least the tide was in their favor. The raft had traveled toward land even when they weren't paddling. Despite the turmoil, the flotilla of rafts quickly approached the shore. Hope swelled in Brazo's chest. If there had been a God, he would have given thanks for that small gift.

Again his unconscious pulled up God. Why? He had seen combat many times before. Even when his fate looked bleak, he never succumbed to praying to a being hiding in empty air.

A raft a good distance in front of them propelled several feet up out of the water as massive crocodile-like jaws sprang to the surface and clamped shut on the screaming crew. Whatever had them was another behemoth in this accursed place. Giants lived under the waters, would giants roam the land?

Ocean boiled as men feebly swam for freedom, and the basilosaurus' jaws snapped for food. It caught a crewman by his legs, and with its head above the ocean, it turned it at an angle and opened its mouth wide. In one gulp the sailor's legs disappeared down its throat. It threw its head back again, and the mouth clamped down on his chest.

The elasmosaurus' head popped up near another raft, and this time its attack was swift and decisive. The prehistoric monster plucked a crewman from his seat in mid-row. The spike-like teeth dug deeply into the sailor's soft flesh. Crushed like a grape, blood dripped down like new wine.

All Hell was breaking loose now.

The giant squid continued to slake its hunger with the United States' finest treasure. The feeding tentacles cut swaths through the ocean and harvested victims as easy a plucking cans off a grocery store shelf.

Just as before, another raft was upended from underneath by a pair of jaws the size of a car.

More elasmosauri arrived randomly in the mix and wasted no time becoming part of the feeding frenzy.

As the flotilla of rafts continued the course, the ocean exploded erratically, like depth charges near the surface. Rafts were being picked off one by one, and the cries of men had become a constant chorus.

It was chaos unknown. Brazo watched as men steadily paddled. He knew they were doing their best to wall off the fear and concentrate only on making it to the objective. The situation wasn't much different than what the soldiers faced on D-Day back in 1944. The men hit the beach in Normandy as a barrage of bullets and artillery shells blasted around them as they advanced. It was one step at a time, one foot in front of the other. Not knowing if the next step was going to be the last. Friends next to you crumpling to the ground after being nearly cut in half from machine gun fire. Body parts slinging blood as the man next to you catches a grenade. War was war. Be it against man or beasts. Right now, in the ocean, the beasts had the advantage.

One of the rafts had made it to shore. Brazo leaned forward in his raft as if to will it to travel faster. *Go, go, go.* His desires were for his men reaching safety first. Yes, he wanted to live, too. Not for a selfish desire, but to know that he had saved as many men as he could. If he could sacrifice his life knowing it would save his men, he would take that offer right now.

His raft moved past an arm cut off at the elbow floating by. The ocean was stained red in splotches. More body parts, deflated rafts, ripped and mangled clothing paved the way to freedom. They were getting closer. Everyone was getting closer to end this madness. But the devils of the deep showed no quarter.

SKEER-AK!

The ear-piercing cry rang from above. A huge, leathery bat-like creature plummeted from the sky and snatched a leg from the surface.

There was no question the dastardly beast was a pterodactyl. The distinctive triangular-shaped head held the leg in its long crocodile-like beak. Its wingspread must have reached thirty feet.

Pterodactyls had been extinct for millions of years. The sea creatures, prehistoric-looking beasts unknown to modern man, feasted up his men. *What was this accursed place?*

Another raft made it to shore. The sailors hurriedly struggled to pull the raft to dry land.

It was a race. Winners got to live, and losers died in the most violent ways imaginable.

SKEER-AK!

The commotion had called attention to more than just one flying reptile. Several more pterodactyls, of various colors and sizes, streaked over from land to enjoy the leftover flesh from gluttonous ocean predators.

Shots rang out as some had to abandon paddles to thwart the aerial attack. Still, more rafts had entered the safety zone. It occurred to Brazo that the rafts, twenty-strong in number when they first hit the water, were now less than half. Even though each raft could hold fifteen men, none of the rafts had been filled to capacity. Small consolation, as the loss of innocent lives, counted well over a hundred.

As Brazo scanned what was left of the flotilla, his men steadily stabbing paddles in water, churning eddies in the sea-green ocean, something emerged behind a raft lagging behind. It was a shark's fin, no mistaking that. The slick, glistening grayish-black dorsal fin rose toward the sky.

The captain's jaw dropped. The fin was as large as a Sherman tank. Looking like a fore and mainsail of a sloop cruising leisurely on a windy day, it quickly closed in on the unsuspecting raft.

Brazo could do nothing but yell a warning and wave his hands. With all the turmoil, his cry was drowned by those suffering into death.

When the megalodon's snout breached the surface, Brazo thought it looked as large as a submarine. A submarine with huge black orbs for eyes and a cavernous mouth filled with unbelievably large, sharp teeth. The knife-to-the-heart-like terror an ordinary shark brings into the unconscious of man was nothing like what Brazo felt now. His sphincter muscle in his backside quivered and threatened to release. He wasn't too proud to admit he knew fear in the past, but this was something unlike he had ever experienced. A feeling he didn't even know was possible. It was as if a thin layer of ice had formed around him and froze him in place. All Brazo could do was stare ahead and wait for the inevitable.

The Reaper's eyes rolled back into its head as if the horrific act it was about to commit was too terrible for even it to witness. Jaws opened wide, then wider, then wider still. Rows of yard long teeth, each sharpened to rival a straight-edge razor, loomed like a bear trap ready to spring.

The jaws snapped shut around the whole raft, and only one edge hung from the side of its mouth. The eight men on the raft vanished in a single chomp. Its jaws went into action, shredding its prey into more digestible pieces. Blood mixed with ocean foam squirted and dripped from the megalodon's mouth before it submerged into the depths.

Brazo felt his spine grow back under his skin. Not far from the giant shark, the ocean turned black. What was this? An oil spill from the *Sutton*?

Turning his gaze, the ocean surface rippled with the giant squid heading away from the feeding frenzy. Had it eaten its fill?

Doubtfully. The shark's unexpected arrival must have put fear in its heart. And why wouldn't it? Brazo imagined that given the choice of small quantities of soft flesh filled with bones wasn't near the delicacy as succulent, meaty squid. Predators and prey. The cycle of life depended on predators and prey. In this case, the squid predator had now become the prey. If only Brazo had some way to deliver a few depth changes or a well-placed torpedo. He would reverse the natural order, and the human prey would become predators!

The raft scrapped its bottom on something. It was the first sandbar between ocean and land. He had become so caught up in watching the shark he didn't realize this nightmare was nearly over. Only two other rafts lagged behind; the others were ahead of him. The winds had become silent of sailors' pain. The ocean no longer boiled with frenzied carnivores, though a few pterodactyls harvested the last remains of body parts floating on the ocean.

"Captain Brazo," Slick said.

Brazo turned his way, eyes heavy from the carnage that delivered the unspeakable violence to his brain.

"We made it, sir," Slick said.

The ocean was shallow enough that Stone bailed off the side and starting pulling the raft to shore. Rodrigue and Underwood went in next, the others followed, with the captain the last to leave. He kept his gaze on the last two rafts until he was certain they were out of harm's way. The whole time he watched, he kept fearing something would rise unexpectedly, and deny one of his men a chance to see the next morning.

Brazo felt the wet sand shift under his boot, and then crunch as he emerged onto the dry shore. The life rafts had been moved away far enough to keep them being pulled out with the next tide. His men looked like they had been dragged by their feet all the way down to the 9th level of Hell.

He stiffened his back and held up his shoulders. Some of his crew stood at attention, hiding emotion as they were trained to do. Others stared blankly into the void. A few cried. A few more lay in crumpled balls as if asleep, or dead—perhaps wishing they were dead.

Fifty-one men, he counted. Fifty-one out of nearly three hundred under his command when they set sail. He had lost over two hundred men and the *USS Sutton* hadn't even been commissioned for battle! Brazo was in charge of the ship's shakedown and he had lost over two hundred men!

He was *the captain*. His men waited for his orders. One man to lead them. The same man who lost two hundred men!

Brazo took a deep breath. He was a natural born leader; from day one in school, he got in trouble for being so bossy to his classmates. The words always came when it was time to command and inspire, but not this time. He went to speak, but it wasn't there; nothing was there.

His face flushed as he realized he was losing control, of his men and himself. Anger swelled from deep inside. He had been put in an unwinnable situation and there was nothing, *nothing*, to do or say to improve the situation.

Brazo turned his back to his men and gazed up at the sky. His right fist came up, and he shook it to the heavens. Several uncomfortable seconds passed, and he said slowly and in a low voice, "Damn, you."

Several more seconds passed. Brazo again said, "Damn, you." His words noticeably louder this time.

"Damn, you!" He had screamed so loud he felt as if he tore his vocal cords.

Brazo fell to his knees and pounded his fists into the sand. He didn't stop until the white sand splotched with red.

CHAPTER 8

The kraken had sensed the megalodon long before it became a threat. There were many other creatures in the vast ocean that gave it concern, but none like the giant shark. The only thing it feared more were the pod hunters.

A basilosaurus might be half the kraken's length, but it was no match for the cephalopod's powerful eight arms. The squid could easily snare the attacker in its long appendages while avoiding its gaping mouth and sharp teeth. And because the basilosaurus was an air-breather, patience assured victory every time. But patience didn't offer the thrill of the hunt. The kraken would waste no time and would feed as soon as it subdued the ferocious sea mammal.

Ocean survival had taught the kraken when food is available, to eat. Indecision or delay of any length might allow the opportunity to vanish. Food was vital for sustenance, but a full belly ensured sharp wits. The kraken's size was a blessing and a curse. Giving it the advantage over the majority of the sea creatures, but making it a large target for those who could do it harm.

The kraken was uncertain about the new food source floating on the water, but didn't hesitate to explore with its long feeding tentacles and sample with its powerful beak. The taste was unlike anything else it had experienced. The meat didn't have the familiar flavor of aquatic pong and eons-aged brine. Instead, the flesh had sweetness and a savory allure that only made it want to consume more.

The kraken knew the megalodon was coming, but it stayed and feasted, plucking humans from the floating devices at will. It didn't leave until the giant shark made its first strike and threatened to come the kraken's way. A quick blast of its ink clouded the ocean, and the giant squid propelled to safety.

The new food was still present. The kraken's instinct pushed it to safety, but its gluttony tried to override.

The *Sutton* rested on the bottom of the ocean not far away at all. The vessel was three times the size of the squid. The strange object had unintentionally become an artificial reef and a perfect place for the kraken to hide until the megalodon ate its fill and left the area. Then, the kraken would return to the feeding frenzy and hope to eat again.

*

The megalodon had left the large interloper with impenetrable skin in pursuit of something that it could eat. The thing that had invaded its territory, the U-boat, was large enough to be a formidable challenge, but never once did it attack or put up a defense. Even when it tugged on an appendage, the worst action the thing took was floating to the surface.

There was no flesh to consume, and the megalodon was hungry.

Sound waves traveled through the ocean, alerting it that food was there for the taking. The shark pointed its nose toward the frenzy and waved its mighty caudal fin, shifting hundreds of gallons of water, and rapidly propelling it the few miles' distance.

It came upon something unknown bobbing on the surface. The body was small enough that it didn't raise any sense of danger. There was only one way to explore, and that was with its teeth.

It opened its mouth wide, then wider, then wider still. It overcame the floating body, and with its powerful jaws, snapped down on it.

The teeth sank deeply into soft tissue, nothing like the other thing that the shark had encountered earlier. Juices rained down its throat, kicking its primordial lusts into overdrive.

Blood.

If it bleeds, it's food.

Instinct overrode reasoning. The shark no longer saw with its eyes. Uncontrollably, its jaws opened and closed. The food squirmed and made loud noises. Bones crunched, but a mass of something remained and couldn't be broken down.

Once the meat was in its belly, the megalodon expelled the mass that it couldn't swallow. No matter, there was still plenty to be eaten nearby.

The ocean turned black as the shark headed for its next victim. It knew the ink as a *sign of a fleeing giant squid*. This squid would rival the shark in size, but not in strength. And instead of a few mouthfuls of this new food source, tons of meaty goodness waited for its taking in the squid.

Its snout pushed through the crimson stained ocean in pursuit. It quickly came over something large resting on the bottom of the ocean. The Destroyer was stationary and didn't seem to provide a threat. The megalodon moved on.

There was blood in the water drifting inland. Squid blood. The beast was injured. Perhaps other predators had found it and were now eating their fill. The shark increased its speed, following the trail of blood.

*

The kraken floated near the surface of the ocean. It suffered severely from the stings hurled from the strange object floating on the water. The attack had caught it totally unaware. The creatures crawling on the surface were easy pickings. Powerless against the hold of its tentacles, and easily cut in two by its beak.

But then the object made loud noises and shards of pain tore into various parts of its body. At first it tried to weather the storm and fight back, hoping to quickly end the attack and resume its feast. Then pain tore through its eye, taking some of the fight out of it.

The object continued making noise, and the pain only increased. With its vision impaired, its instincts took over, and the squid headed out to sea to heal.

The kraken knew it was weak and smelled its blood leaching into the green ocean. There was nothing to do but wait.

Vibrations in the ocean warned it something approached. It positioned its eye in the coming direction, but the injury had it at a disadvantage. Still, the unknown sea creature came.

A quick blast of ink erupted, and the squid mustered the energy to use its arms to propel away. It noticed weakness in its flight. That wasn't good. The predator continued in fast pursuit.

With no place to take refuge, the kraken dove for the bottom of the ocean. Darkness would offer some cover, and it would use the advantage of millions of years of evolution to blend in with the surroundings. It didn't take any energy to rest in one place, and it hoped to go unnoticed.

*

The megalodon followed the blood scent, and then felt the ocean move as the kraken shot out its ink and sped away. The hunt was on, and the shark increased its speed.

The squid was nearby, and the blood trail now led toward the bottom.

Deeper and deeper the megalodon went. Light was almost nonexistent, but its eyes functioned well enough that nothing would go unseen.

There it was, the giant squid. Injured, but whole. The shark didn't know what happened and didn't care. There was a great feast to be had, and no other predators had arrived yet to share in the spoils.

The megalodon circled above the kraken, just out of reach of the feeding tentacles.

The squid sensed it had been discovered, and went from being as stationary as rock, to unfolding with its head up and raised arms, swelling its body to maximum size.

The shark continued to circle, and the kraken turned its body to keep its eye on it, an ancient dance where only one would survive.

In an instant, the megalodon made the first move and dove with uncanny speed toward the kraken.

The kraken reached one feeding tentacle from the side and tried to wrap it around the shark. Then, it shot out more ink and jutted from the bottom.

The megalodon felt searing pain as the tentacles' suction cups embedded into its skin. It quickly turned its head and tried to bite it, but snapped just inches away. The other feeding tentacle came unexpectedly from the other side around its back. While it still had the advantage of speed and mobility, the shark whipped its tail from side to side, breaking free of the kraken's grip.

Wasting no time, the shark maneuvered behind the kraken. As a feeding tentacle sped through the water in defense, the shark opened wide and bit down on it. Blood gushed, sending billowing blackish-red clouds. It chomped down one mouthful, then another, and then the appendage severed in two.

The remaining feeding tentacle latched on to the megalodon's tail and pulled it down. The kraken reached up with its other eight arms. Three found purchase and pulled the shark into its clutches. The beak opened wide, and a chunk off the megalodon's side went missing.

The shark thrashed erratically about until finally breaking free. A blast of black again darkened the water. The squid might be injured, but it still had a lot of fight left in it.

It was time to make a difference. The megalodon swam away a short distance and waited for a clear shot at the kraken. When its eye faced the other direction while looking for the predator, the shark swam in and bit down on its mantle. Its jaws went into action, chowing down on as much of the rubbery flesh and as fast as it could. Arms and tentacles reached up to pull it away, but the megalodon shook them off until satisfied it had done significant damage before speeding away.

The shark watched as the kraken's flaying arms slowly lost life. In desperation, the giant squid opted to leave the depths and head to the surface.

The kraken drifted upward, and the megalodon struck again, this time tearing into the last feeding tentacle, and ate without resistance. It had won!

Tons of fresh meat was there for its taking. More than it could eat at one time. More than it could eat in five different times.

Mouthful after mouthful filled its belly.

Something wrapped around the megalodon's back and all the way under its belly. Before it could turn, the tentacles tightened with such force, the chunk of kraken in its mouth jettisoned out.

Another kraken had arrived, perhaps its mate. This squid had no injuries to weaken it for battle. The other eight arms took hold, and soon, the megalodon was completely at its mercy.

The megalodon was trapped, unable to move anything other than its snout and bite at empty water.

The kraken waited for oxygen-rich water to enter the megalodon's lungs, and when it expelled from the gill slits, it tightened its grip.

The shark redoubled its efforts to escape, but it was just as useless as before. It struggled to fill its lungs, and when it exhaled, the grip tightened again.

Unable to breathe, held in a death grip by a massive cephalopod, the megalodon went limp, never to swim the savage oceans of Earth again.

CHAPTER 9

Artur Phelps held a bosun position on *U-616*. His training made him a master of all things vital to keep a sea vessel in proper working order. It was he who planned the daily work assignments and supervised their operation. With so few men on a submarine to pull duty, he worked as hard as the others when it came to executing tasks. Twenty years a member of the *Kriegsmarine* had practically replaced the blood pumping through his heart with the ocean's brinish water. Right now, leading four men on a recon mission in a jungle so thick at times they couldn't see beyond one meter in front of them, he felt like the proverbial *fish out of water*.

Seniority aspires many unwanted privileges, he thought. Which didn't surprise him, as the go-to man often dealt with the unforeseen. But that involved things of the sea and ship operation. Four men followed in his footsteps, each depending on him for their safety.

"I have not seen anything this thick since I spread the thighs of a *dirndl* girl named Heidi, after retiring from a long night of drinking at a Bierpalast," Wilhelm Lange said, parting broad foliage with the barrel of his *Sturmgewehr* 44. The man supported more girth than a typical crewman aboard a U-boat. Dense whiskers covered his round face, hiding his upper lip.

"I am surprised you can see anything at all through those eyebrows," Roland Gwerder said, the next man behind him. "Perhaps you should use your bayonet to shave. On second thought, do not. You might dull the edge."

"How about I dull the tip of my bayonet by poking you in the ass?" Lange said. He paused and scratched his chin. "On second thought, maybe not. I hear you like things poked in your ass."

Gwerder rolled his eyes. "With you, it's always about sex. With the men, with the women, with animals, with inanimate objects—why is everything with you about sex?"

"Eh? I'm a torpedo man. Every day I have to service one torpedo to make sure it is in proper working order. With my hands, I must carefully wench the long, hard torpedo over to the service bench where I check the batteries and hand wipe the outside skin clean. My job reminds me so much of handling my massive *schwanz*," Lange said.

"Really, Lange. Gwerder is right. Everyone thinks you are a sexual deviant. It is time you grow up. We are tired of hearing about sex in every conversation," Ernst Ziegler said. His eyes squinted behind glasses. A sharp nose and two large front teeth that lips didn't fully cover gave him a rodent-like appearance.

"Ernst, you too? We have been friends for many years," Lange said, hurt in his tone. "The fact is that I am so lonely for my wife. All I can do is think of her—day and night. You know my wife, Ernst. You have been to my house, planted your feet under the dining table. You know my wife has big tits. I can't stop thinking of her big tits. You have noticed her big tits, right?"

Ernst raised a hand. "I do not want to talk about Anna."

"We are not talking about Anna. We are talking about her tits. She has a nice rack. You would agree?"

"Lange—" Ernst started.

"Wide across her chest. Nice, *big* breasts," Lange continued, he reached out a hand and massaged empty air. "You had to notice her tits."

"Okay, if it will shut you up. *Yes*, your wife has big tits," Ernst said.

"Hey! Why in the hell were you looking at my wife's breasts!" Lange said, his eyes narrowed.

"I—"

Before Ernst Zeigler defended himself, Fritz Witt said, "Knock it off, you two. You are distracting from the mission." Witt was an engine room mechanic. He was below average height, and his small-in-size hands gave him advantage working in tight spots. The man wasn't known for his sense of humor, of which he had never appeared to have.

Phelps knew he had let the banter go on too long, but his heart just wasn't in leading the men into the vast unknown. His compass worked, and he did know how to use it. But the thought of mapping an area until nightfall and returning the next day seemed too dangerous. At least if they stayed with the rest of the U-boat crew, there would be safety in numbers. But the commander had sent two groups of five, the other led by Jakob Norz, about on their own. What if they came upon one of those flying reptiles they saw on the beach? They were well-armed, and he hoped the rifle rounds would be powerful enough to take one down if needed. Still, a pterodactyl in 1945? What other surprises might lie in wait?

"Hey, look. Over there," Gwerder said.

All gazes turned to where his rifle barrel pointed.

A few meters away in an unusually clear space, a small creature curiously observed them as it sheltered behind a large leaf.

"Ah, it's nothing but a lizard," Lange said.

"But its *neck*," Ernst said. "It is too long."

"Okay, then it is a long-neck lizard that lives on this island. If it scares you, I'll be happy to shoot it in the head," Lange said.

"No one is shooting anything," Phelps said. "We are only two hours into our mission, and we cannot afford to give away our position. The commander believes Americans from the Destroyer may have made it to land, too."

"I bet it is those things we keep hearing scurrying about," Witt said.

Something rustled behind the compsognathus, scaring it to leave its cover, and dash off to safety.

All five men watched the escape, and then turned mindful expressions toward one another.

"Did you see that?" Ernst said.

"I believe we *all* saw it," Gwerder said.

"A lizard that walks on two legs," Lange said. "It lost its arms and learned how to walk without them. I saw a dog once who did not have front legs. She got around well when she had to."

"That lizard ran like it did not need front legs. I doubt it ever had them. And the tail, did you see the tail?" Phelps said. "It was a third the size of its body—like it balanced the front end. This is not some ordinary lizard."

"I think you are right," Witt said. "This is a strange land we are on. The pterodactyl at the beach should have prepared us for more unusual creatures. If you think about it, that animal most resembled a dinosaur than it did a lizard."

"A dinosaur?" Lange said. "It is too small to be a dinosaur. Dinosaurs are big." He spread out his two arms, holding the rifle in one hand. "Some are the size of tanks. Some are as large as a house."

"And some are as small as a chicken, like the one who was watching us," Witt said.

Well, this was certainly a situation Phelps considered but had hoped to avoid. *Dinosaurs*. His mind called up images of large theropods terrorizing the land, mighty ornithopods grazing—some armored like any modern day mechanized vehicles, and giant sauropods lumbering through the landscape.

He looked at the four others with him and at their puny weapons. Facing animals from the prehistoric past was an encounter he didn't want.

"Perhaps we should head back to camp. Inform the commander of our find," Ernst said.

"We tell the commander a two-foot lizard scared us back to camp?" Gwerder said.

"It is not a lizard. It is a dinosaur," Ernst said. "We must warn them to expect the worst."

"We are not abandoning the mission with such little reason," Phelps said, although if he wasn't in charge and held accountable, he might have made the same suggestion.

"Dinosaurs lay eggs, right?" Lange said. "Roosters don't have penises, but ducks do. Have you ever seen a duck *schwanz*?" He had directed the question to Gwerder.

"No, I cannot say I have ever had the pleasure," Gwerder sarcastically said.

"It is like a corkscrew. I would hate to be on the receiving end of that," Lange said as he twirled his index finger upward. "What about a tyrannosaurus' penis? How big do you think they get?"

"I bet it is at least large enough to fill your mouth and shut you up," Gwerder said.

Before Lange had a chance to rebuff Gwerder, Phelps said, "This foolishness stops now. Everyone check your weapons and be ready for the unexpected. If you see something, do not shoot unless threatened. If there are dinosaurs, I am not even sure our rifles are enough to stop them."

"The Americans. What should we do if we come across the *Americans*?" Witt asked.

"If we see them before they see us, we do nothing. We will map their position and return immediately to camp. The commander believes the Americans may outnumber us three to one," Phelps said.

"*Scheiss-Amis*," Lange said with disgust. "If the odds were five to one, we are strong enough to win the fight."

"The odds have always been against us. But even our superior intellect and technology can only accomplish so much. We are in a strange land, and our resources are limited. We have to be careful and not over extend ourselves...not like the *Führer*," Witt said.

"Do not speak ill of the Führer," Lange threatened.

Witt held an icy gaze on Lange. "The Führer is dead because he did not realize Germany's limits. All that he gained is now lost. We have escaped with little more than our lives. I will always be a proud German, but I do not intend on extending the dreams of the Third Reich."

Lange looked like he wanted to say something. The man was obviously conflicted. Hitler's defeat, Germany's loss, all children of the Fatherland carried the bitter taste in their mouths. It was difficult to admit defeat while air still filled the lungs.

"We cannot change what happened in the past, and the future depends on what we do now," Phelps said. This was no time to mourn what might have been. "Let's move."

*

Phelps cautiously led the four crewmen through tall grasses and around mighty trees with odd-shaped leaves. Plants with tall, woody trunks dotted the landscape. Their crowns consisted of what looked like long, stiff leaves. On closer examination, the *long leaves* were constructed of smaller leaflets to the main stem. One thing for sure, Phelps learned not to brush against the leaves. A close encounter with his left arm drew blood and still itched.

They had come across more of the small dinosaurs, though the *two-legged lizards* kept their distance. Strange reptile-looking birds would take to the air when they approached, sometimes startling he and his men. Pterosaurs, much smaller than the ones on the beach, nested in trees high above. The flying reptiles made a noise that sounded like a cross between a hoarse crow and a throaty monkey. None of the indigenous life presented a threat thus far.

The men had stayed relatively quiet, each sorting out the hand fate had dealt.

Phelps often thought of fate, the mysterious chance of the when and where a person was born. He had been lucky to be born of Aryan descent and considered it a privilege. But what if he had been born as French or even English? Certainly, he would be proud of his roots, but it would be in ignorance. All other races were inferior, some more than others. What if he had been born a Jew? Or in Africa? He couldn't imagine looking in the mirror and seeing a black face staring back at him.

Despite everything he believed and held dearly to, the fact remained that Germany had all but lost the war at this point. The rest of the world would lord over them—perhaps even more so than after the Great War. What if the concentration camps were kept open and the German people were herded like animals waiting for the slaughter? The notion seemed *inhuman*. Yet, Phelps realized that the inferior would think the same thing of their people.

Something died inside him at that moment, but a seed from deep within sprouted. *Perhaps we are not all that different from one another after all.* Phelps suddenly felt small, insignificant. Almost that his whole life had been a total waste and it was pointless for him to continue on.

He looked back at the faces of his men. Surely they harbored similar feelings on some level. But men were forced to play the *pride* game. Don't show emotion. Don't share feelings. Keep that stone-like façade and carry on as if nothing else mattered than the mission.

Phelps took a deep breath and pushed on. They hadn't eaten yet and still had plenty of water. It was hot, but the jungle did provide ample shade. At least the jungle wasn't as dense now. In fact, they had been traveling slightly uphill, and now the terrain was leveling.

The grass grew lower and trees thinned enough that Phelps didn't feel like something waited to attack at every step.

A tannish-yellow pterosaur soared down from above and nested at the top of a tree. This reptile was much closer than the one at the beach, though not as large. Phelps estimated its wingspan to be a little more than three meters.

All the men watched in fascination. The pterosaur had a long and somewhat narrow bird-like beak. They were close enough, or at least the teeth large enough, for them to see. It was a strange sight, as Phelps imagined what birds back home would look like with teeth. The crest on the back of its head was as nearly as long as its bill. The creature looked like a strange mixture of bat, bird, and reptile.

"I wonder if it sees us if it will attack," Gwerder said.

"It would be the last thing it would do," Lange said, bringing up his rifle and taking careful aim. "That head would look good on my wall."

"You don't have a wall to put it on," Ernst said.

"I will one day. I will send for Anna once I make a new life in South America. We will live on a farm, have many children." Lange lowered the rifle, his eyes glistened. "Our kids will only know the future I make for them."

So, Wilhelm Lange had a heart hidden beneath his brash behavior. Losing the war apparently had him reconsidering everything he believed in and forced him to take a different perspective in life. Phelps found that to be true of himself. Time and fate would write the others' stories.

"Look over there," Witt whispered.

Something wandered into Phelps' peripheral as Witt spoke. At first, he thought it was a rhinoceros. A greenish-yellow rhinoceros. But it didn't take long for his brain to override the false imagine it had initially forced. This was no rhino from the wilds of Africa. This was another dinosaur. A triceratops, as he recalled from his schooling. Beyond that, he didn't remember much about the animal. This one was more than two meters long and a meter and a half tall. It was a strange looking creature, as its shape resembled four-legged mammal grass eaters, but had a beak-like mouth instead. Two brow horns set above its eyes, and a smaller horn jutted from its nose. A bony frill fanned atop of its head. One thing for sure, the animal would have made a good battering ram.

The triceratops grazed lazily on the green grass and occasionally sampled leaves from nearby plants. Its stumpy legs kept it naturally close to the ground.

The five men watched from behind a broad leaf plant.

"This could be a problem," Phelps said in a low voice.

"I am sure the commander would want to learn of this as soon as possible," Ernst said.

"It is a grass eater, so I do not think it would see us as food. Still, it might consider us as a threat. I am not sure of its skull thickness. Bullets might have a hard time finding its brain," Witt said.

"Then we shoot it like a deer—behind its front legs," Lange said.

Witt shook his head. "Its body is so thick. I am not sure if the bullets would penetrate far enough reach its heart."

"As long as we keep quiet and our distance, we will not need to find out," Phelps said. But what if the triceratops *did* find them and attacked? He realized that wishing to avoid an encounter was not what a leader should do. It was his job to prepare the men for the worst. "We are going to go around it. If it discovers us and attacks, everyone take the best shot you can. We do not necessarily have to kill it, just scare it off."

Heads nodded in agreement.

Just as Phelps was about to make the first step to lead his men, something far away *thumped*. He froze and turned an ear toward the sound. The thump repeated. Did he just feel a vibration on the ground at the same time as the thump?

The time between thumps shortened, and there was no doubt at each sound the earth beneath his feet shook. Something large was coming their way.

A gray head emerged past branches of a tree some thirty meters in front of the triceratops. The T. rex stepped confidently toward its prey.

Phelps felt a cold tingling sensation where his spine connected to his head. This was what he had feared the most. A dinosaur five meters tall and over ten meters long approached with uncanny grace. It had grayish skin similar to an elephant's, with darker stripes running from its spine down its side. Two small arms bounced in front of its chest, and the tail shifted to balance its body as powerful legs tread across the earth.

The triceratops listlessly raised its head with its mouth open. It immediately saw the T. rex heading for it and turned to escape.

Something rumbled behind the triceratops, blocked from view by jungle growth.

A few moments later another triceratops emerged. This one all brown in color, and three times the size of the previous one. It ran toward the T. rex like an angry bull toward a matador.

The T. rex checked its advance and veered to the side. It opened its monstrous mouth, showing rows of sharp, jagged teeth, and hissed.

Phelps and the others watched in awe.

Phelps was astounded by the sheer mass of these two creatures. The triceratops wasn't as tall as the T. rex, but it was considerably longer. And even though the triceratops didn't have teeth, from what he could tell, its beak looked like it could cut the rex's leg in two with one bite.

The T. rex side-stepped and hissed again, shifting its body about, threatening to attack.

The triceratops held its ground and brayed as loud as a train whistle. It lifted its head and pointed its brow horns at the rex.

The death dance began with the T. rex stepping toward the grass eater and biting empty air near its head. The brow horns narrowly missed the rex's mouth, and the animal stepped back in a defensive move.

Trying to get a rear advantage, the rex started to circle the triceratops. The grass eater was considerably nimble for its size and spun on its five-toed feet to keep its armored head pointed at the predator.

The rex lunged again without teeth finding purchase. But the triceratops jutted its head forward, digging its horns in the rex's gut.

With arms up in surprise, the rex thrashed its head and tail about enough to wiggle free. Red blood oozed down the side of its stomach where the horns had penetrated.

The air was electrified by the savagery. Phelps could hardly breathe from the firm hand of fear's grip. For a moment, he thought the rex might be on the retreat, but the creature had simply turned in a short circle, and brought its mighty jaws across the triceratops' head.

Spikey teeth chomped down on one of the brow horns, the triceratops struggled to pull free. The rex didn't waiver and held fast through the cries of its victim, twisting its head about until the horn snapped in half.

Backing away, the triceratops kept its head up, warning the rex it wasn't ready to surrender the fight just yet.

No matter. The rex dove with another crushing bite that came down on one side of the prey's frill. Sharp snaps of bone breaking penetrated the brays of the grass eater. Somehow it managed to free itself once again, but its movements were less certain. There was no mistaking the triceratops was injured, and the rex acted like victory was only a matter of time.

Another bite toward the triceratops' head had it twisting to the side to avoid it, leaving the back of its neck exposed.

Wasting no time, the rex's jaws opened wide and bit behind the frill. Blood squirted like a fountain. The triceratops cried as loud as an air horn and thrashed as much as its squatty body allowed.

The rex held firm, twisting its head from side to side until the grass eater went still. It pulled back and came away with a man-sized hunk of blood-dripping meat. Lifting its head back, the dinosaur swallowed the first spoil of its kill and returned to strip more flesh from its victim.

"I think we should leave now," Witt whispered in Phelps' ear.

Phelps had been lost in the fray. Witt's words pulled him back to take charge of the situation. He turned and looked at the faces of his men, their thoughts easily read. "We are heading back to camp."

They wouldn't be able to make it to camp before dark. Still, beasts this big didn't seem to inhabit the span of land from where they were to the camp. Even making it back halfway would give him enough confidence they would be safe for the night.

CHAPTER 10

Brazo stared past the sand he knelt on trying to see into a dark future, but there was nothing. Still breathing heavy from his outburst, he tried to relax the muscles in his tight back. He slowly realized the spectacle he'd made of himself and felt the eyes of his crewmen upon him.

How could he have lost control of himself in such manner? Rage had totally consumed him and became his master. Was he fit to command anymore? Even harboring such doubt was enough for him to step down and let the XO take over.

"Captain?" Slick asked, concern in his tone.

Brazo raised his left hand and waved him off. He *was* the *captain* and would remain as such. Standing to his feet, he brushed embedded grains of sand from his skinned knuckles. His shirt had become untucked, and he methodically pushed the tails back in his trousers. Facing his crewmen, with an unapologetic expression, he said, "Our mission is to set camp, and then try and figure out where we are and how to contact help. We are members of the United Sates Navy, and I have the utmost faith that all efforts to find us will be exhausted. Now, I'm not going to lie to you and say getting rescued is a certain possibility. There is so much we don't know, but if it's one chance in a million, then it's still a chance. We'll have to keep our wits sharp if we want to survive this thing. You saw what we faced in the ocean. I imagine whatever lives on land will be equally as deadly. Somehow this land has escaped the passage of time. If any of you remember reading about dinosaurs from school, well, hope for the best, expect the worst." His last warning seemed absurd to his *own* ears, but he was in no position to take chances.

The crewmen's reactions varied. Some gazed around in disbelief; others received it as ordinary orders. At least everyone was on their feet. Those traumatized the worst had pulled themselves up by their bootstraps, though tears did roll down a few faces.

"We lost a lot of good men today. I am the captain, and I take full responsibility. I grieve for them just as you. But now isn't the time to wallow in grief. Distractions will only get us killed. I don't want to lose any more of you. Stay tight, watch out for yourself and others. We'll get through this together," Brazo said.

He turned to the XO. "Have the men gather supplies from the rafts and prepare to find a good location for camp."

"Yes, sir," Slick said and turned to the crewmen. "You heard the captain, empty out the rafts." He turned and pointed. "Rodrigue, you and Underwood grab a couple of rifles and scan the perimeter of the jungle. Let us know at first sign of trouble."

The two gave a quick *salute* and sped away toward their guns.

Slick looked down at the sand, and then back toward Brazo. "Captain?"

Brazo felt a little sorry for what he imagined weighed on his XO's mind. The two had grown close enough during a previous deployment to say they shared a genuine friendship. The captain could bulldoze through the event to his men like it never happened, but Alan Slick, his friend, wanted closure.

"Yeah, I lost it. I can't say it any other way," Brazo said.

"I'm trying to hide it, but I'm still shaking inside," Slick said. "What we went through was totally unbelievable."

"It was, but our training prepared us for war. In a sense, this isn't different. This is *prehistoric war*. It may be a war mankind wasn't meant to fight, but we have no control over our situation. It's up to me, it's up to you, and every *water dog* in our crew to make this work. I know I let my emotions take over earlier, but I've learned from that. That's a line you won't have to worry about me crossing again."

"I know you, Captain, and I have the utmost confidence in your command," Slick said. "Still, if there's anything you ever need to unload, I'm here."

"Alan, you've always been there for me." Brazo placed a hand on Slick's shoulder and patted it twice. "Don't worry, what doesn't kill me only makes me stronger."

"This isn't nineteen forty-five anymore, is it?" Slick asked.

"My gut tells me *no*, as ridiculous as it sounds."

Slick exhaled slowly, and said, "Well, we got here somehow. So, there should be a way to get back."

"Let's hope so. I know that storm had something to do with it."

"I've never seen a storm like that before," Slick said.

"There're a lot of things here we've never seen. A storm like that might not be a rare event."

"Still, if another storm came up on us, would it return us to our time?"

Brazo said, "If there is a God, then *yes*, I believe so." He gazed sternly into Slick's eyes. "I *have* to believe so."

***

Camp was set a couple of miles inland. Brazo chose the area because the jungle thinned out enough to give them mostly an unobstructed view several yards in any direction. There were still enough tree limbs and plant foliage to construct temporary shelters. Plus, a small stream in the area would provide fresh water once they ran out of their emergency supply.

Traveling through dense jungle to get there had been arduous and had everyone's nerves on end. Most of the time, the low foliage was so thick it was impossible to see what was three feet to any side. Two-legged lizards, he had to force his rational mind to accept as *dinosaurs*, would run when come upon, scaring everyone half to death. Brazo was surprised no one had pulled a gun and taken a shot. Other creatures, hidden but not far away, plodded through the jungle. His imagination ran wild with what terrifying meat eaters might charge and wreak havoc. Fortunately, none had.

Reptile-like birds made strange noises and fled. Small pterosaurs took refuge high in trees. One urinated on a crewman behind him, missing Brazo by inches.

Each life raft held emergency supplies enough for fifteen men. Nine rafts had made it to shore, so food and water at this time weren't an issue. There were C ration biscuits, cans of chewing gum, candy, vitamins, Chocolate tablets, milk tablets and pemmican. Brazo had eaten pemmican before, and it was far from a food favorite. The concentrated mixture of fat and protein provided much-needed calories for survival, though.

Other supplies included rope, hatchets, fishing line and hooks, cups, flare guns, a survival radio, and flashlights, of which none worked.

There were enough M1 rifles for every crewman to have. Fortunately, in addition to the ammo each raft contained, two of the rafts loaded with extra ammo and grenades miraculously survived the journey.

Brazo watched his men busily at their tasks. Each seemed to immerse themselves in their work to wall off any of their fears.

A few men hacked low-lying tree branches and dragged them over to others. These men used hatchets to strip leaves and offshoots to form imperfect poles. The branches then went to be used as the framework for a teepee structure. From the looks of it, each shelter would be large enough to house five men comfortably. Long leaves similar to a banana plant's foliage went on the outside for shielding.

There was enough rope to secure the crown of the structure, but one crewman had found vine suitable as a replacement. Brazo admired the sailor's efforts to conserve resources and believed the young man would have a bright future in the US Navy. *If we make it back to our time again*, he thought, reality a constant reminder of their strange situation.

Brazo had assigned Jim Stone and another man to the survival radio. The radio wasn't made for two-way transmission, only as an emergency beacon. It had a hand crank and only two tubes, of which were broken, but the spares had been intact. Stone had it repaired quickly. As the crank was turned, a distress signal in Morse code automatically transmitted across the 500-kHz international distress frequency. For maximum range, a kit providing a balloon and a hydrogen generator allowed the antenna to be floated up as an aerial wire.

"We'd have better results if those two sailors were churning ice cream," Slick said; he had walked up while Brazo was lost in his thoughts.

Brazo chuckled. "A dish of cold vanilla would be good right now."

"I'm a chocolate man myself."

"What gets me is that this radio only sends out a distress signal. There's no way for us to know if anyone picks it up. We could do this for hours, days, weeks, and never know. Protocol demands we make the effort, but right now…right now I'm not sure how much *Navy protocol* applies."

"I think I know what you're saying," Slick said.

"Our rules and regulations back in our time had specific purposes. But now some may need to be modified in order to preserve resources. I'll let the men take turns cranking the radio for the next couple of hours. By then it'll be getting close to dark. The shelters will be finished, and we'll sit down for chow. You need to assign the men to guard duty, and then everyone needs to get as much rest as they can. We've had a trying day. The men are in an automatic mode right now. Work is keeping the demons at bay. But tonight, those demons will all come back as they lay their heads down. It's a process that they…*we all* will have to go through. But once sleep comes, the healing process will continue. I want the men in the best shape possible."

"Understood, sir," Slick said.

"We're used to life aboard a ship. Being out in the wild with sailors with a hodgepodge of skills has taken them out of their routine." Brazo turned his gaze to the ground. "Wagner, Mitchell, Edwards, Perry, Philips, Harris… I can't believe we lost every other commissioned officer," his voice trailed. Lifting his head back up, he said, "We'll pick leaders from the chiefs and petty officers after chow. We're going to organize according to strengths. A structured command is imperative to our survival."

"I couldn't agree with you more, Captain," Slick said. "I've already been thinking ahead of you. With fifty-one men, I figure we can assign ten or so each to one leader. Three groups will be assigned to camp operations, the other two will split security and recon duties. Of the base groups, one group will be responsible for finding food. One will be responsible for preparing food, and the other general camp maintenance."

"Good, good, I like the way this is shaping up," Brazo said. "Right now, I think we stay here for a maximum of two weeks. Unless a miracle occurs and we're rescued, I'm going to move us to higher ground. As we paddled to shore, I noticed the tallest point north of here. It's going to be a hike, but we can learn the most about our situation from up there."

"We could always send a recon team out," Slick said.

"We could, but I wouldn't want them that far away without backup. If there're more dangers out there, I want all of us to be together in the fight. To win, we'll need all the numbers we have. You know what we faced in the ocean. I'm sure you've considered what we may find on land."

"All the life we've encountered so far hasn't proved much of a threat. Maybe animals on land are different. Maybe evolution on land here is different than in the ocean."

"Sounds a lot like wishful thinking," Brazo said. He looked around. "Large animals would avoid dense jungles. Something the size of a T. rex needs real food, not something the size of a banty rooster. Big dinosaurs would live in areas not as dense even as we're in right now. And big dinosaurs need to eat other big dinosaurs."

"Understood," Slick said. "One last thing, before I go check on the men. The Germans, if they're here, what about them?"

Brazo slowly nodded. "Indeed...*what about the Germans*?" His voice had faded in the end.

*

Rodrigue and Underwood had paired up when the XO assigned eight crewmen to help guard the perimeter while the other crewmen were busy setting up camp.

Adam Rodrigue had been a church-going boy whose father taught him the difference between right and wrong from the time he was in the cradle. Growing up in the '30s had been tough in Thibodaux, Louisiana, on the banks of Bayou Lafourche. The sugar cane industry had steadily declined over the years, and his father had resorted to hunting and fishing to provide his family food and income.

Adam had been a curious child and had chores suited for a boy well above his age level. His father rose well before the sun came up, but Adam would always be at the kitchen table right after the first pot of coffee came off the stove to share a cup.

His father taught him how to tie a clinch knot on a hook and how to tease the fish into taking the bait. By the age of five, Adam had his own .22 rifle. The gun was a single shot crack barrel, and his first kill had been a beaver. His dad hated beavers. The pests constantly blocked streams and threatened their property with flooding. His mother had used the tail to make soup with egg noodles and peas.

By the age of ten, Adam could disassemble and reassemble his dad's 3.3 HP Evinrude boat motor. There was no task he was too afraid to try and learn. Even welding, which didn't prove to be one of his better skills.

Education had been secondary to learning life skills. Still, he had mastered math basics and understood fractions and decimals. He was told his reading level was a couple of grades behind, but so far, as long as the words were in English, it hadn't proved to be much of a hindrance.

Adam looked over at Danny Underwood and wondered what was going on in his buddy's head. He didn't know much about Danny, other than he was from New Orleans and looked to be a few years older. So far, he hadn't made an effort to talk to anyone about the horror they just went through to get here. Was Danny scared? The man didn't show it. Adam had felt a burning pit in his gut ever since they reached shore. There were parts of him that felt numb. It took concentrated effort to keep his wits alert, pushing the images of his mates torn apart from his own mind.

"What are you staring at?" Danny asked. He was around ten feet away, leaning his left shoulder against a tree.

The black cloud of Adam's reverie dissipated, and Danny came into focus once again. "Uh, nothing. Just thinking."

"Better keep your eyes moving. You want to live, don't you?"

Adam quickly looked about, fearing his lack of attention had put them both in danger.

Several minutes went by without anyone saying a word, then Danny said, "You look kind of young to be in the Navy."

"I didn't feel too young, until today."

"I'm twenty-two. Been in for four years now. I've seen some action." Danny dropped his gaze. "Nothing like today, though."

"I'll turn eighteen in a month. Seven months in, stateside. The *Sutton* is my first deployment."

"*Seventeen.* You must have lied to join up."

"No, the recruiter knew I was seventeen. My dad signed the papers to let me join."

"Your dad? Man, he must've wanted to get rid of you."

Adam shook his head. "No, it wasn't like that. My *Uncle David* died in Normandy storming the beach on D-Day. He..." Adam's voice broke. "He was my *Parrain.*"

"*Parrain,* that means Godfather. You must be *Catholic.*"

"I am," Adam pulled out a medal of Saint Valerie from under his shirt and rubbed his thumb over it.

"How many Hail Marys did you say while the monsters were attacking us?"

"I lost count."

Danny laughed. "I don't think much about religion and stuff. But if that's works for you, it's a free country."

"Yeah, and I want to make it a free world, too. I was so mad when I got the news Uncle David died. He never married or had children. So, I guess he thought of me as his own. He joined the Army wanting to put a stop to Hitler and Mussolini, and gave his life trying. I had to badger my dad and mom day and night for two months before they agreed to let me sign up with the Navy."

"Your Uncle David sounds like a good man. At least you know he didn't give his life in vain. Hitler and Mussolini are both dead, and it's men like him who allowed the Allies to kick the Axis' butt in Europe."

"Yeah, just as soon as we finish the job in Europe, I'm gonna get transferred to the Pacific. There isn't ever going to be peace until we kick the dog out of *all* our enemies," Adam said.

"Can't let the Japanese beat us. They'll make us start eating raw fish heads," Danny said.

"I can't—" Adam stopped mid-sentence as something rustled a fern in his peripheral. He darted his gaze over to it and brought the barrel of his M1 up to waist level.

There was nothing there. It could have been just the wind, but an inner voice didn't believe so.

Danny was on full alert, and hurriedly brought his rifle to his shoulder as a reptilian bird hiss-cawed and bolted from a nearby branch.

An eerier stillness fell about. Adam looked over at Danny for direction, but the man seemed just as unsure as he.

After several minutes had passed, Danny relaxed and rested the rifle stock on the ground.

The knotted muscles in Adam's back loosened, allowing him to expand his chest and take in a deep, refreshing breath of air. Staying this on edge all the time was exhausting. His mind drifted in anticipation of his watch being over, hoping for the cool of the night and a place to lay his head to ease in blessed relief.

A head poked through fern leaves a few yards away. It took a moment for Adam's eyes to take focus. At first, the head didn't look real. The head reminded him a grass snake's, but it was larger than a German Shepherd's head. It opened its mouth, and instead of a forked tongue coming out and tasting the air, it showed rows of leaf-shaped teeth. The eyes appeared large for its head, and penetrated deeply into Adam's alert gaze, setting off every danger signal in his brain.

The head disappeared, rocking the fern as it made its escape.

He brought his rifle up, but there was nothing to aim at.

Danny took two steps closer, and whispered, "I saw it too. What was that thing?"

"I dunno. I don't know much about dinosaurs. That one didn't look too big."

"Well, it didn't stick around. Maybe it's more afraid of us than we are of it."

"You think?" Adam said, hope in his tone. He craned his neck as far as he could to see beyond the foliage. "Well, I guess it's gone. We—"

Danny cried out in surprise.

Turning, Adam saw his crewmate face-down on the ground and being pulled backward by a dinosaur that had him by his left foot. The creature in many ways looked like a larger version of the smaller dinosaurs they had encountered on the way to camp.

Directly behind it, another of its kind waited to join in on the feeding. Long, slender legs with raised sickle-shaped claws on the inside of feet gave it a bird-like appearance. The head and body were all reptilian, though, stretching at least six feet in length, and over three feet in height. Its olive-green skin had golden stripes marking its spine.

Adam raised the rifle and fired at the troodon holding Danny in its tooth laden trap. The bullet ripped into its left side and knocked it off balance. The other beast brought its small arms into its chest and cocked its head back in surprise.

He fired again, striking the wounded attacker where the heart should have been.

The dinosaur dropped, and its companion backed away.

Before Adam could get off another shot, something hooked into his shirt above his belt, digging past the top layer of skin and pulling him off balance, down to the ground on his back.

Golden eyes with curved, blade-like pupils loomed above a troodon's open maw. It struck snake-like for his throat.

Adam barely had time to bring the M1 over between them. The dinosaur's jaws snapped down on the rifle's stock and steel barrel instead of his soft neck. The troodon uttered a raspy hiss. Bits of teeth chipped off and hit him on the cheek.

Danny started screaming latticed cries of pain and not surprise.

Stealing a quick glance, Adam was horrified seeing three troodons had Danny surrounded. One had him by the left leg, another, the right arm. His rifle lay useless on the ground. Adam could do nothing but watch as the third troodon raked the sickle-shaped claw across Danny's abdomen. Blood, intestines, and assorted viscera belched out over his thighs.

Adam's pulse throbbed in his ears, rhythmically blocking Danny's shrill shrieks of agony for far too brief of moments. His crewmate was getting slaughtered, and he was in the fight of his life.

The troodon gave up on biting through the rifle and retracted its head. Adam wasted no time in bringing the butt of the rifle over and smashing the dinosaur on the side of its skull. The blow was effective, as it staggered sideways, giving him time to roll over to his feet. Bringing up the gun, he shot the troodon in the chest before it had a chance to attack.

Danny's cries had given way to sickening sounds of teeth ripping into raw flesh and guttural grunts, as chunks of his body disappeared down the troodons' throats.

Two more troodons appeared from behind the feeding frenzy. Apparently, they didn't want to share in the kill, and instead, preferred a fresh one for themselves.

The two separated and came toward Adam, cautiously stalking in an attempt to surround him. The wounded troodon's left arm had gone limp, but it still had plenty of fight left in the rest of its body.

There was more commotion behind Danny. An unknown number of troodons headed toward the camp! Adam prayed the gunshots had everyone on alert and ready to fight. He was in no situation to warn them. In fact, unless he acted quickly, he would share Danny's fate in a matter of seconds.

The rifle went up, and he fired two shots into one troodon, two shots into another, and one more into the wounded one, who keeled over dead.

The other two hissed and snapped into empty air but didn't go down.

Carefully aiming this time, he squeezed the trigger, only to hear a dull *click*. Out of ammo! His clip had failed to eject, reminding him he was empty.

Sensing the advantage, the two wounded troodons advanced toward Adam.

Instinct took over, and Adam spun around on his heels and ran in the opposite direction. Fear gave wings to his feet as he fumbled to remove the M1's clip. He didn't know how fast the dinosaurs could run, especially now that they had been shot, but through fleeting glances backward, he knew they struggled in pursuit. He zigged and zagged, doing his best to lose them.

Time lost all meaning at first. All his mind knew was to keep running and never stop. Jungle foliage became a blur. His feet went up and down, each inch hopefully pushing him from harm's way. He ran and ran, too scared to stop in case they were right behind him.

A wall of thick brush veered him off his path to offer cover after maybe a good quarter hour of fleeing. He smashed past a scrubby bush, not feeling the cutting leaves on his arms until he was well past them. The skin would grow back. The pain didn't matter. If the dinosaurs got a hold of him, it would be the end.

He had fished an ammo clip from his pocket between strides and racked a bullet in the chamber. In this thick brush, it would do him little good to lie in wait as the dinosaurs would have to be on top of him before he'd see them and get off a shot. Too close for comfort. He needed to reach an open area and find a place to hide, take them out as they exited the brush.

He put both arms up and pushed past a large palmetto. His foot came down on empty air and Adam lost his balance, tumbling down the side of a steep hill.

The foliage wasn't near as thick there, which was a disadvantage. More plants would have helped to break his fall. Now, he struggled to hold on to his rifle, roll down the hill, and keep from twisting a foot or breaking an arm. He narrowly missed smashing into a tree trunk. Over and over, down he went on a wild rollercoaster ride.

Finally, after a descent that seemed like it would never end, the land flattened out, and he rolled to a stop.

The next few moments he lay still, cautiously testing various parts of his body to measure injury, but keeping his gaze on his surroundings in case more predators were in the area.

As near as he could tell, there was nothing worse than scrapes and bruises, although a couple of his ribs on the left side might have been cracked. Still, nothing that would put him out of commission.

He pushed himself up from his hands and knees, and then picked up the rifle. At this point, he was so turned around he wasn't sure which way was camp. How far had he run? It couldn't be that far as a crow flies, but heading in any direction other than the right direction, would be disastrous.

Surveying the area, he realized a gully at least fifteen feet wide stretching as far as he could see to either end hindered him from traveling north. He walked over to the gully and saw the walls of either side dropped off some thirty feet.

There was one advantage. A medium sized tree had fallen some time ago and lay across the gully, acting as a natural bridge. Its branches had long since rotted off, and Adam questioned its integrity.

One of the troodons following him poked through the foliage at the top of the hill. This surprised Adam, thinking his shots would have done more damage. It didn't make the same mistake as he and slowly stepped down the hill.

The other troodon arrived, and now two were coming for him.

No matter, he had eight fresh bullets and several more clips in his pocket. He would wait for them to get a little closer and take them out like ducks in a shooting gallery.

Just as fast as his confidence grew, it came all crashing down. Five new troodons emerged to join the wounded.

The odds were no longer on Adam's side. It was unlikely he could get in enough successful shots before succumbing to the hungry mouths of the dinosaurs.

He looked over at the tree spanning the gully, feeling a little light headed as death quickly approached. Running over to the tree, he hopped on the three-foot diameter trunk, and stood on wobbly legs.

The troodons were close enough that he could hear the clawed feet kicking up dirt and the hisses of anticipation.

Adam held the M1 in front of him like a balance pole and began to step across the tree.

At first, he put one foot in front of the other, trying to keep his gaze across to the land on the other side. He imagined that if this tree had been lying on flat ground, he could have run across it. But it wasn't, and heights had always made his knees weak.

One step was a little less than sure, and he almost lost his balance. His butt felt like it rose up and stuck in his throat. He steadied himself, and now led with his left foot only, inching his way across the tree, his right foot trailing his left in measured steps.

A troodon arrived at the tree and hissed loudly.

The hairs on Adam's neck bristled. For a moment, he thought he felt its hot breath. But that was just his imagination. He had to maintain control and concentrate on his walk, not the danger that he *prayed to God* wasn't capable of following.

More troodons arrived. He felt them strike the tree with their claws and bodies, not knowing if it was out of frustration or if they were so angry they were trying to knock him to the depths below.

Were these dinosaurs smart enough to work together like that? He hoped not, and just wanted them to leave. What would he have done if they *had* followed him across the tree?

Just a few more steps, and then just a couple of more. Soon his foot found solid ground, and he quickly brought the other by its side. He had made it!

Turning, he saw the seven troodons snaking their heads back and forth, obviously frustrated.

One of the wounded could barely stand. It listed to one side. When it reached its limit, its left leg collapsed, and the beast tumbled down into the gully's darkness.

Adam considered taking careful aim and killing as many as he could, but then thought better. He was safe for the moment. Firing his weapon would only signal his location to other creatures in this land. That, he didn't need.

He could either go north, east, or west. After a quick *Our Father*, he pointed his nose west, heading toward the ocean, and begin walking.

CHAPTER 11

The spinosaurus' eyes opened as warm sun rays cast orange-yellow blades past thick foliage of the jungle. Rest was essential, recharging its energies to hunt, feed, and ward off any threats stupid enough to intrude on its domain.

Short, muscular legs with mighty thighs stretched out, extending talon-like claws from four webbed toes as it arched its back. The tail, half its body length, curled upward until the tip nearly touched the middle of the sail shrouding the dorsal spines.

It had spent most of the morning navigating the fresh waters of a lake, its long crocodile-like head floating just above the surface, taking in air through two small holes closer to its eyes than the end of its snout.

The successful hunt provided a sturgeon some ten feet in length, filled with rich eggs. Later, an alligator gar fish wandered too close to its conical-shaped slanted teeth and took residence in the spinosaurus' belly. Despite the near five hundred pounds of food it had eaten earlier, its twenty-one-ton mass craved more.

Twisting its body to get its legs underneath it, its two short arms with blade-like claws useless to help lift itself, the spinosaurus rose to its feet and stretched out its long neck.

The beast was a magnificent sight to behold. Fifteen feet tall and nearly fifty feet to the tip of its tail made it the largest theropod prowling the land. Black splotches darted its gray-colored back, just below the seven-foot sail edged in red.

It turned its head and looked about. This area was its kingdom. It had come at a cost, but the spinosaurus didn't have to pay as dearly as those he defeated in battle to take it.

Its violent existence started from the time it opened its eyes and would end only when they closed the for the final time. That's the way it was on this land. Once out of the egg, running for its life, small enough for practically any predator to catch and eat. As it grew, it learned to travel in packs with its own kind, bringing down prey in coordinated attacks for all to share in the feast.

Now it no longer needed the support of others. Its ferocious reign had it commanding an area vast enough to provide food until the end of its days.

The breeze carried the sharp tang scent of a fresh kill, triggering strands of drool past the teeth of its long jaws. *Red meat.* Not the soft flesh of fish, which cut in half with but a single bite. But coarsely grained meat that teeth *pushed* through; sinew held muscle pouring bloody nectar across its tongue. Meat that had to be torn out in chunks and filled the belly with satisfaction that lasted far longer than any flesh the waters had to offer.

Its mouth opened, and it hissed in anticipation. Energized by its savage nature, the spinosaurus plodded toward the recent kill.

*

The spinosaurus neared its destination and spied a T. rex feeding on a triceratops. The rex was large, but nothing the king of the land felt it had to fear. This was its land, and the spoils of any kill were its to take.

The four-toed feet stomped across the earth. Each step shook the ground, announcing its arrival. There would be no sneaking up on the rex to surprise it, and there was no need too. The spinosaurus would claim the triceratops, and if challenged, the T. rex would suffer the fate it deserved.

As the spinosaurus approached, faint spore from another creature mingled with the meat scent. The smell was unlike anything before, not as pungent as other animals in the land. This only made the spinosaurus angrier, as an unknown interloper had dared to invade its kingdom.

The T. rex stopped cold as its head pulled back, attempting to rip out another mouthful of meat. It knew the spinosaurus had more than curiosity. It was here to take the prize the rex fought to win.

Not breaking stride, the roar from the spinosaurus warned the T. rex to leave. Leave or face the same fate as the victim lying on the ground.

Slightly deeper in tone, the rex opened its mouth and matched the ferocity in a roar that indicated that it wasn't going to back down.

No matter, the choice cuts of the triceratops had been consumed. The flesh of the T. rex would be as tasty. The thrill of the kill would make the spinosaurus savor it all the more.

The rex stepped from the side of the triceratops to the front and dared the spinosaurus to come closer.

Closer it did come. The dance of death began anew. A dance between two foes with only one possible outcome. There would be no question of the mightier in the end. It was winner take all, even the flesh of the victim.

The spinosaurus slowed its advance, turning its head on its long neck, trying to make its opponent guess from which direction it would strike. It cried a warning, giving the rex one last chance to reconsider. Leave now or face its wrath.

The rex, perhaps drunk with the victory of its earlier kill, stretched out its neck and repeated the warning.

Throwing the first blow, the spinosaurus swung its head to the side, crashing jaw to jaw with the rex. Then, it attempted to latch its interlocking teeth at the end of its snout onto the rex's neck.

The rex crashed its head down on the snout and managed to latch its jaws on part of the spinosaurus' neck instead.

A surprised hiss-roar cut the jungle air. The spinosaurus frenziedly shook its head and brought its tail over, smashing the rex in the side and knocking itself free from a threatening grasp.

Before the rex had the chance to gain its balance, the spinosaurus head-butted the rex and sent it backward.

The triceratops was directly behind the rex, and the theropod lost its footing and fell to the ground.

Giving the enemy no quarter, the spinosaurus lowered its head and chomped down on the T. rex's throat.

The T. rex roared and futilely slashed empty air, trying to reach the neck with its sharp claws attached to hands on arms too short.

The spinosaurus knew it had the advantage, all it had to do is wait. Pain throbbed in its throat where the rex had bit him. This made it even madder, and it brought its jaws together even closer.

The rex's feet came up, and its claws ripped six-inch cuts in the spinosaurus' neck. The blow was severe enough that the attacker let it go, and the rex up-righted itself.

Blood poured from the spinosaurus' wounds. Blood poured from the T. rex's, too.

RRRAGGGGGUHHH! a third road thundered through the air.

The spinosaurus and T. rex turned their attention from each other to face the new challenger.

A green carcharodontosaurus, latticed in yellow, boldly joined the fray. The beast was larger than the T. rex and only slightly smaller than the spinosaurus. Its head was considerably bigger than either of the other dinosaurs and had serrated eight-inch teeth lining its jaws.

The spinosaurus stepped toward the challenger. This was its land. It was the king. All would back down in fear or become food for its belly.

SEEESSSARRRGGGGGAHHH! the spinosaurus returned.

Bounding without hesitation, the carcharodontosaurus butted its blunt head against the long spinosaurus face. Neither gave way, and each took turns snapping empty air in an attempt to get the advantage.

Blood continued to pour from the spinosaurus' wounds, perhaps fueling the carcharodontosaurus' confidence.

In a surprise move, the T. rex had maneuvered behind the spinosaurus and sank its teeth in the meaty portion of the body between the tail and the fin.

Instinctually, the spinosaurus whipped its head to the side in an effort to pull the T. rex off. In its haste, it exposed its neck to the carcharodontosaurus.

The mighty beast took advantage of the spinosaurus' poor decision. Its massive jaws clamped down, driving spike-like teeth into flesh and striking bone.

The spinosaurus, weak from battle and loss of blood, felt its life force slowly drain away. It was held at both ends, unable to move. Its tail was not powerful enough to break it free.

Air barely had passage to fill its lungs. Its heartbeat pulsed where teeth met flesh. The once and powerful king felt a weakness unknown. Reality slowed. The light filling its eyes dimmed. A calm washed over it, quenching the fires of its lifelong savagery. Darkness brought peace, and peace, death.

*

The carcharodontosaurus held tightly to its victim until the legs gave way and it sank to the ground. The champion dinosaur opened its mouth and roared in victory.

The T. rex released its hold of the back, raised its body, and faced the winner. Blood still dripped down its neck; its face ragged from battle, and chest heaving for air.

A penetrating gaze was the only threat the carcharodontosaurus offered.

The challenge not accepted, the T. rex turned and slunk away into the jungle for the healing powers of nature to care for it.

The land had a new king crowned on that day.

CHAPTER 12

U-boats generally carried rations designated to last twelve weeks. It was traditionally true that German U-boat crewmen ate the best food of all the German forces in the war. Christoph often wondered why this was so but never enquired further. Perhaps it was because U-boats offered the poorest living conditions. Crewmen weren't allowed to bathe or shave. They were allowed only the clothes on their backs and one change of socks and underwear. Hot bunking on cots increased in grime and human filth every day.

As commander, he was the only crewman afforded privacy. His small quarters, located next to the command room, hid behind a thin curtain. The curtain did almost nothing to block out noise, but still, it was nice not to look out of the bunk and see the nonstop daily activities around him.

For *U-616*'s final mission, the U-boat had been inadequately supplied with quality foodstuffs. Its hasty departure didn't allow much of the usual fresh meats, vegetables, and breads, which were practically exhausted, onboard. Instead, an ample amount of tinned meats, preserved fish, dried potatoes, rice, noodles, and *Bratlingspulvera*, a soya-based filler, was available and in quantities to last five round-trips to South America. At least they wouldn't go hungry for a long time.

"Did you enjoy your supper, Commander?" Lt. Gunter Bach asked as he approached from his side.

Christoph sat on a rather large branch that had fallen from a tree. Night had descended, and a small campfire burned a meter away. The flames' dance reflected off his pale white face. Melanin in the skin needed sunlight to darken the pigment. U-boat crewmen weren't known for their tans. "Yes, I had a filling tin of meat and two biscuits."

"Beef or pork?"

"Pork flavored salt," Christoph said.

Bach chuckled. "I had the beef. My stomach is full. There are worst things than German canned rations. Have you ever eaten any Italian rations?"

"You mean *Mussolini's ass*? Yes, for two weeks one time. I think I lost ten pounds during that period."

"We called it *old mule*," Bach said.

"That is an insult to mules. I would think a *mule's ass* would taste better than the canned swill the Italians make," Christoph said.

"If we don't find any fresh food to eat here the whole crew will become constipated."

"I wish I could say with confidence that we will not be here long enough for that to happen. I am eager to learn our recon parties' reports tomorrow. This is a strange land. But if we could find civilization of some type—a primitive village, people who could give us an idea where we are. If they had boats, then there is a chance we can find our way off here," Christoph said.

"*If* we are in nineteen forty-five," Bach said.

"Yes, if we are in nineteen forty-five," Christoph tiredly said. "I vacillate between two trains of thought. One, that we are on an undiscovered island, and the other, that we have traveled through time. The former gives us a chance, the latter...." his words faded. "I do not know how to deal with the latter, so my mind gravitates to the hope we are still in our time."

"What if the recon parties find nothing but more jungle?"

"Then I'll send a group out on a different mission. I'll have them go to the highest point in this area—that small mountain to the north. I'm hoping to learn more of the Americans. Phelps' group should scout near their position. I would prefer not to engage them, as it could jeopardize the mission. They could outnumber us. If the Americans appear to be a threat, we will discuss our strategy with the SS officers."

"What if the recon parties don't come back?" Bach asked.

Christoph admired Bach's candidness. Losing one or both of the recon parties was a possibility. He could tell Bach had been a little uncomfortable with his decision to send two parties out at the same time. Ten men comprised one-fifth of his crewmen. Even losing five would be a crushing blow. If facing the Americans in all-out war, they needed every rifleman available. "I will deal with that question only if it becomes a reality."

"Understood," Bach said, swallowing the bitter response.

Christoph didn't mean to react so coldly, but the truth was he was just in no mood to anticipate defeat. "I was wondering, if the men on recon fire a rifle, what is the maximum distance away that we could hear it?"

Bach thought a moment, and said, "Hard to say. Wind conditions play a part. It mostly depends on the terrain and the amounts of trees and foliage. I would think five to seven kilometers at best, but it is probably much less than that."

"Well, I will take the fact that we have not heard any gunfire as a good sign."

The fire flames had diminished somewhat, and the hot embers glowed like the sun on the horizon. A minute or two of silence had passed before Christoph asked, "Something else on your mind, Lieutenant?"

"Yes, sir, there is. The crewmen. I had heard some murmurings on the boat before, but the men are speaking a bit more openly now."

"What is the concern?" Christoph asked.

"This mission. These men had no say in the matter. They were forced to leave Germany and move to South America. Yes, some were pleased. Many were more concerned about their families at home."

"But once in South America, they can start the process of bringing family over."

"There is no guarantee and no way of knowing how long that process could take. But it is more than that. Commander, Hitler may be dead, but the war is not over. Some believe we act like cowards, running to South America, while the *Kriegsmarine* still battles the enemy."

Christoph stiffened his back, and through gritted teeth, said, "We are *not* cowards. We are loyal members of the *Kriegsmarine*, and we follow orders. No matter what the orders are. If we are ordered to stay in the war and fight to the death, then we would complete that mission. In this case, we are to land in South America and integrate into different societies. *U-616* is to be secretly moved to a Brazilian Naval base where its future has been marked *classified*."

Bach remained silent for several moments as the crackle of burning wood filled the background. In a low voice, and in an even tone, he said, "Some believe all but the members of the SS will be killed when we make land."

"What? That is nonsense," Christoph sprang off the fallen tree and stood. "No German loyal to the Fatherland would commit such an atrocity."

"The concern is the SS members are fearful of being discovered once making land. What if one of the crewmen assimilates into a village and then is later discovered to be a German refugee? Does the man trade his knowledge of the most sought after SS elite for a chance at amnesty?"

"I am a member of the SS, and I have no knowledge of such a plot," Christoph said.

"You are a commander in the *Kriegsmarine*. The others were Hitler's close associates. You, and Erik, and the rest of us, may be among those who are targeted to die."

"I—"

"Frankly, Commander, I do see this as a strong possibility. These are desperate times. Eichmann, Barbie, Mengele, and Stangl, will be among the highest war criminals sought after. They all have proved to be mad with power. The lengths they may go to protect themselves may have no limits."

Bach's words shined light on dark truths. A sinking ship always proved a man's true character. These were men who had seen so much death, but it had bothered them less than a change in the weather. Would the loss of forty-five German lives only be seen as a means to and end?

"Lieutenant Bach. We cannot allow something as nefarious as you suggest to take place. It would violate every oath we have taken to the Fatherland. Such a ruse would come from desperate men, as you say, outside of the order we have pledged to uphold."

"What should we do, sir?"

"We will watch, observe, look for any hint that such a plan is in the making. If we discover it to be true, then I cannot guarantee our guests will make it to their desired destination. We may very well fail our last mission."

*

Erik Neuzetser had eaten his supper in front of a small fire, sitting by his dad on a tree limb.

His dad had little to say as they ate, and Erik even less. The conversation they had earlier, as Erik helped clean and load rifles, only added bricks to the wall dividing them.

There was nothing new in his father's words of encouragement. He had heard them hundreds, if not thousands, of times before. Repeating the same thing over and over served no purpose. Erik *understood* the points his father taught. But for him, things in life weren't so *black and white*. There was much gray to many issues.

Erik thought his *own* father would be at least one person in the world he could confide in. His doubts about the war, the treatment of Jewish people, his desire to study abroad when he was old enough. He wanted to see the world, meet real people of foreign lands. Talk with them, share ideas, share their native food. He wanted to go to Africa and meet black people in a village, see the pyramids in Egypt, the Great Wall of China, and the Indians in the East and West. He couldn't accept the world was as he was taught.

History had been one of Erik's favorite subjects in school. Things he knew of the world today didn't match with some of the historical accounts he had read. His teachers, his father, everyone harbored their own biases. Erik had a mind of his own, and he wanted to formulate his own opinions; set his own path in life.

Things his father wanted for him in life weren't bad. They might have been fine for his father and others, but not him. He hated that he couldn't be the ideal child who was the pride of his father. But being true to himself, even if it destroyed him, was more important to him than anything.

Erik had departed his father's side when he finished eating to find Blondi, Viktor's German Shepherd, and give her the portion of meat and biscuits he had left over.

He arrived through the darkness near the cave housing the patients. Blondi wasn't far from the opening but out of sight, lying on her stomach with her head resting on her front legs. She stood with slight difficulty, favoring her hips, and sat.

"Hey, Blondi," he whispered and patted her head. He didn't know if Viktor would have a problem with him feeding her and certainly had no intention of asking permission.

The dog responded by licking his wrist.

Scooping some meat on a biscuit piece, he fed it to her.

She happily downed it and anticipated more.

The other members of the SS were in the cave with Viktor, who was speaking to them. Erik's skin crawled on the back of his neck as he heard the man's voice. Viktor's voice was stronger now and resonated with a cadence all too familiar.

He continued to feed Blondi, stepped a little closer to the cave's opening, and listened.

"—unacceptable. We were to be in Brazil in two days," Viktor said.

"I assure you the commander is managing the situation as well as possible," Dr. Mengele said.

"We are truly in a compromising position," Stangl said. "The U-boat is beached. The radio is not working. We are in a place not even on the map."

"Franz, you are not making the situation more palatable with your whining," Eichmann said.

"We will learn more by noon tomorrow. Two parties were deployed to search the area. Perhaps they will find a means for us to escape," Barbie said.

"I need to be in Brazil in two days!" Viktor demanded. It had sounded like the man pounded the ground with his hand while he spoke.

"Two days, two weeks, the only thing that matters is you arrive safely," Mengele said.

"No!" Viktor said with disgust. "I want to be there when it happens…."

A few seconds of silence passed.

Barbie asked, "What are you anticipating?"

"Revenge," Viktor coldly said.

Silence parted discourse once again.

"Revenge? How?" Barbie asked.

Viktor evilly chucked. "The war is not over. Germany is not defeated, despite the Allies' advance. Germany's day is yet to come."

"Perhaps you are tired," Eichmann said. "Dr. Mengele, can you give him something to help him sleep?"

"I will sleep when I am dead. And I am far from being dead," Viktor said. "Listen, listen all of you. The Third Reich has maintained secrets within secrets, within secrets. In a few days, two US merchant vessels will arrive off the US east coast. The *John Carver* is destined for New York City, and the *Black Point* will travel the Potomac River and reach Washington, DC. Each carries an atomic bomb capable of mass destruction. The United States will collapse after the attack—thrown into total chaos. But revenge doesn't stop there," Viktor said, growing excitement in his tone. "*U-234* is on a course for Japan. Aboard is a complete atomic bomb and enough uranium oxide and heavy water to build three additional bombs. I have provided them with the plans necessary to construct more. Japan will cripple the rest of the world and bring it to its knees. The emperor has agreed to share in the spoils of war. Germany will rule Europe and the Soviet Union, they will take the East and the Americas."

"I...I had no idea we were that far along in our nuclear program," Barbie said.

"I was so looking forward to supervising gauchos on a beef ranch," Stangl said. "I guess I will have to be content slaughtering animals of the two-legged variety."

"Stangl, I find your prater disrespectful," Viktor said.

"I'm sorry, *Mein Führer*, no disrespect was meant," Stangl said.

CHAPTER 13

Hampton Wallace and Joey Gridley held perimeter watch of the camp some fifty yards away from Rodrigue's and Underwood's position.

The first rifle shot cracked the air like thunder, sending electricity up Wallace's spine. He jutted his gaze over to Gridley, whose eyes grew wide.

They lowered their centers of gravity and held their rifles at the ready. A quick scan found no danger.

The second shot had them both running toward the sound. Rodrigue and Underwood were under attack.

Wallace held his rifle to the side as he dug his boots into the ground and dodged plants. Running toward an emergency was totally opposite of human nature. Part of his training included firefighting; engaging, rather than fleeing, a fire on a boat. It was one of the hardest things he had to overcome.

Heading toward a fight, rather it be warships on the ocean or submarines beneath the sea, was really no different. In those cases, though, if you didn't win, you were more likely to die than not. After all he had been through today, Wallace knew he wasn't ready to die.

Six more shots led him to his crewmates' location. Wallace arrived first and put on the brakes as he came upon a body lying on the ground being torn to shreds by three troodons. The remaining scalp covered with sandy blond hair identified the sailor as Underwood.

Gridley almost crashed into Wallace as he stumbled to a stop. The young man gasped when he saw the gruesome sight, and then sounded like he fought to keep the contents of his stomach down.

One troodon raised its head curiously over at the two humans. Its face was smeared with blood and chunks of raw flesh wedged between its teeth.

Another troodon chewed greedily on an intestine, which hung from the side of its mouth.

The third hissed out a warning, and then turned away from the kill to ward off any potential thieves.

The threat snapped Wallace to attention. He lifted his rifle and shot the troodon twice in the chest, and it lunged for him.

The other troodons left the feast and charged toward Gridley, who, by that time, made a feeble attempt to bring his rifle up.

Wallace hit his back on the ground as the weight of the troodon overcame him. He yelled, fearing the teeth and jaws of the dinosaur that rested on his chest, inches away from his face.

Gridley fired hastily, both shots missing their target. The two troodons pulled him to the ground. One chomped down on his throat, stifling a scream into a raspy fight for air.

The troodon on Wallace's chest was limp. The bullets had done their job. With some effort, he pushed it off his body. Rolling to the side, he carefully aimed and shot the dinosaur clenching Gridley's neck, just a few feet away, in the eye.

The troodon's head jutted to the side, letting go of its stronghold, and then it collapsed.

Wallace rolled to his knees and fired three bullets into the troodon contemplating to attack. Again, another kill.

With heart pounding and chest heaving, Wallace's eyes immediately told him his was too late to help his crewmate. *Poor, Joey. He didn't deserve this*, he thought.

Shots erupted, coming from the campsite. Wallace looked around for any signs of Rodrigue but saw none. A dead troodon a few yards away could have pointed in the direction that Rodrigue might have run.

Gridley was dead. Underwood was dead. Wallace could only hope Rodrigue had somehow escaped and was circling back to camp.

For now, there was a war going. He again found himself running toward a challenge where the consequence of losing was certain death.

*

Sailors busily about camp froze in place at the sound of the first rifle shot.

Brazo and Slick had joined in on erecting the latest teepee, laying supporting tree limbs used for sides to center point.

Jim Stone walked the perimeter after the supports were in place, wrapping the rope below the crown. The structure was surprisingly simple but strong.

Brazo had turned and scanned into the direction of fire when the second shot followed. "Trouble," he said to no one. "Men, get your guns!" he ordered.

The M1s had been laid across stripped tree branches to keep them off the ground near the middle of camp. Crewmen dropped hatchets and whatever else they were carrying to arm themselves.

"Let's go, men. Let's go," Slick said. "Get your rifles and some spare clips."

The first few did as they were told, and then turned to face Slick.

More shots fired in the distance, coming from the north.

"Okay, once you have your weapon, I want everyone to form a line crossways. Keep three feet between you. We're going to fan out and march toward the shots," Slick said. "Come on, move it! Our guys need us."

Brazo had heard an M1 discharge enough times to know that it was one of his crewmen's weapons and nothing of German origin. There was little comfort in that thought, as he'd much rather face the enemy he knew over anything resembling the beasts in the ocean.

He waited for the last of the men to pick up their weapons before getting his. There were still a few grenades left, so he grabbed one and clipped it to his belt.

His men had dutifully formed a line, though Slick had reassigned some to step a few paces to the rear. The XO realized a line of over forty men would spread them too thin.

"Okay, men. Keep an even pace," Slick said. "Stone, lead us forward."

"Yes, sir," Jim Stone said. The man was near the center of the line. "Let's go."

The men stepped at a quick pace heading toward the battle.

Brazo considered taking the lead but was unsure how the men would hold together. They weren't used to land maneuvers, and he wanted to keep them in line, watching them from behind.

Foliage wasn't too thick, but there were enough obstacles between plants and trees to separate the men more than he would have liked

"Douglas! Go the other way. Stay with the group," Brazo yelled at a crewman to the left. "I don't want—"

A scream from the far right had everyone stop. Men in line on that side scattered.

Brazo saw the disruption but couldn't see what had caused it.

"Look ahead! They're coming!" Stone yelled.

From the distance, Brazo saw a pack of two-legged dinosaurs in a loose group charging their way. These creatures were about half as tall as a man, but their long tails and necks made them appear larger, more of a threat.

Stone let one rip from his M1, leading a cacophony of firing rifles.

Brazo hurried to the line only to crash into a crewman who was back-peddling. Both hit the ground and scrambled to their feet.

The first troodon led two others past one side of Stone, breaking the line. Stone managed to drop one of them, but the others kept running.

Brazo dove to the side as a crewman spun around and fired, narrowly missing being shot.

The crewman froze for a moment when he realized how close he came to shooting the captain, but then fired again.

Men screamed, guns fired, dinosaurs screeched. The wall of crewmen collapsed in chunks as a horde of troodons blanketed the area.

One sailor had lost his gun but managed to get the inside of an elbow around a troodon's throat in a firm choke hold. For the moment, he was able to keep away from the sharp teeth. To his fortune, Slick arrived with a drawn .45 and put four shots into its chest.

At least bullets were deadly enough to kill. Brazo fired three rounds at a dinosaur that snapped at a crewman whose M1 had ejected its clip after missing his last shot. The captain made his first kill.

Two troodons had knocked a sailor down and commenced ripping him to shreds with the claws on their feet. The beasts didn't have the mercy to end the man's life before eating him.

Attacking head-on, a troodon bit a crewman on the throat, and when the unfortunate soul pulled away in retreat, his larynx remained in the creature's teeth. Blood poured down his chest like a crimson waterfall.

It was difficult to know how many creatures were on the attack. Brazo estimated over fifteen. From his vantage point, he saw four creatures dead, as well as eight of his crewmen. This was brutal, savage war. This deadly land offered no quarter.

Brazo continued to target and fire as troodons presented themselves. It was tricky business, as the beasts were on the constant move, and he was in fear of hitting his shipmates.

A troodon charged from one side. Brazo fired and missed, and the ammo clip sprung into the air. He had no time to reload and fled in retreat.

The troodon *hiss-cried* in pursuit.

With the dinosaur on his heels, Brazo dropped to the ground and picked up a hatchet one of his men had discarded. Blindly, he swung his arm around and narrowly missed the troodon's head as it lurched for an attack. The near-hit spooked it enough to momentarily retreat. Brazo hopped up and slashed the air between them back and forth, hoping for an opportunity for the blade to meet skull.

Weaving its head like a boxer in a fight, the troodon, too, waited for a chance to connect.

Unexpectedly, the troodon switched from snapping at his head, and instead bit the back of the hatchet as it *swished* by. The hatchet ripped from Brazo's hand.

The captain stood empty-handed, feeling like a naked child in front of a starving lion.

Before the events of his life could flash through his mind as he anticipated death, two shots rang out from behind.

The troodon toppled to the ground.

"You okay, sir?" Hampton Wallace asked.

"Yes, son," Brazo said as he turned and saw his savior. "Fine shooting. There's more!"

Wallace lowered his head, and with defiance in his eyes, sped toward the fray.

Brazo retrieved his rifle and fed the clip.

The crewmen had gravitated into bunches of a few men each. This gave them extra firepower and didn't present as many friendly targets getting in the way of the enemy.

It immediately became clear to Brazo that his men had endured the storm. Only a random shot went out here and there, from areas he couldn't see.

XO Slick saw him and hurried in his direction. "You okay, Captain?"

"By some miracle, yes," Brazo said, surprise in his voice.

"This was bad. Really bad," Slick said.

He had counted eight men dead earlier. What was the total number now?

Men that had been run off from the group's center started arriving, many with dead bodies in tow. This had been a deadly fight, but his heart already knew that.

What disturbed Brazo the most was the horrific damage done to his crewmen. Most of their wounds were life-threatening. One bite from the sharp teeth could cut deep enough to sever arteries. The claws on their feet could eviscerate a man in one swipe. These weren't the largest of creatures, probably weighing not much over a hundred pounds. But, pound for pound, he didn't think anything from 1945 could match their deadliness.

Those who had guarded the camp's perimeter had left their posts to join in on the fight. Now, all the men gathered around their fallen brothers.

"Is this everyone?" Brazo asked.

"Yes, sir," Slick said.

"No, there're two more," Wallace said. He lowered his head, and said, "Gridley…Joey and I heard the first shots and ran to help. We found Underwood. They got him before we got there. Those things attacked and killed Joey before I could stop them." Wallace raised his gaze and sighed. "Rodrigue wasn't there—he was teamed up with Underwood. There were two dead dinosaurs there. One by Underwood, the other a few yards away. Rodrigue may have had to make a run for it."

Brazo nodded. He hoped Rodrigue was alive and they would somehow find him. There was no way, with all the losses today, he was going to risk any more of his men to leave and search for the missing man. He counted the bodies, and two crewmen checked for vitals, which by the looks of things to be a total waste of time. *Thirty-three*. Thirty-three more men dead under his command, *all in the same day*.

"Listen up, men," Brazo said. "We have met the enemy, and we have won. Victory was at the greatest of cost, but we did what we were trained to do. Our training kept us alive, and it will keep us alive." Brazo made every effort to maintain a steady tone, without callousness, and with concern. Men with zombie-like stares looked in his direction. He didn't know if they had the capacity at this point to even hear him. "I have decided that staying here for the night puts us at more of a risk than I'm willing to accept. We'll give our men a shallow burial and move out before dark. I want to be far enough away from the carrion eaters, who are sure to come, so we won't have to deal with them. We'll take our chances for the night. Again, I'm in command, but I can make no promises. When we wake in the morning, we're heading north to a high point. Hopefully, we'll get a better lay of the land and find a way out of this accursed place." Brazo gazed over to Slick and nodded.

"Okay, men, let's grab the shovels and get to work," Slick said.

"Uhh, Greene's not dead," one of the crewmen examining the bodies said.

Brazo and Slick walked over to the fallen sailor. The man's torso had been ripped open, and half of his organs had been eaten away. His chest barely rose and fell.

"I don't know how he's alive," Slick said. "Captain, there's no saving him."

Brazo rubbed his eyes, leaned back his head, and said, "The XO is going to lead all of you back to the supplies. I want you to get a drink of water and the shovels. Am I clear?"

Perplexed expressions looking back at least told him they understood his order.

"Executive Officer, Slick. Lead them away," Brazo said.

"Fall in!" The XO headed for the supplies.

Brazo watched his men wearily turn and follow, continuing the be the good sailors they were trained to be.

He waited until the last in line was barely out of sight before he removed the Colt from his side.

*

Jim Stone poured water from a container. He had filled everyone's cup, with Slick being the final one served.

As they drank in silence, the shout of a Colt .45 honored the life of the latest fallen sailor of the *USS Sutton*.

CHAPTER 14

Jakob Norz had been reassigned by Commander Christoph Neuzetser from electro machinist to leading four other crewmen on the recon mission mapping the north. He wasn't sure why he was chosen to the lead the group. Perhaps it was his age, as he was among the oldest of the crew. Of the crewmen he led, they were all at least twenty years his junior. Norz had the reputation of being a perfectionist and demanded the same from others.

The five were on their way back to camp after spending the first night near a wall of limestone. He estimated they had traveled over twenty-four kilometers before bunking down. During the journey, they had seen creatures out of time that staggered the imagination.

The first they came upon was near fifty meters long when it walked on all fours. Which at first sight seemed impossible because the front legs were shorter than the rear, resembling arms more than legs. But that didn't stop this duckbilled beast from getting around. It had a crest on its head that went down the neck all the way across its back, where it became noticeably taller. Norz thought its body shape resembled a teardrop turned on its side, the point being the tail. The massive creature must have weighed several tonnes. Standing on four legs had its head taller than an average man. When it stood on its back legs to eat leaves, Norz guessed it towered another three meters!

From the looks of things, this animal was a herbivore. Which gave Norz some relief, as he questioned how effective bullets from his *Sturmgewehr* would fare against it.

Along the way, they saw a few more creatures like it and some similar but distinctly different. There was one four-legged creature that reminded him of an armored vehicle. The beast was five meters long and two meters tall. Its back had raised plates that might have been strong enough to stop bullets. At the end of its tail, a mace-like ball attached to the end, a defensive weapon for certain. A similar animal, a stegosaurus, grazed listlessly as they made their way past. *Stegosaurus* was one of the few dinosaur names Norz knew, and right now, he wished he knew them all. Pterosaurs, as well as the small two-legged dinosaurs, were so common that they no longer looked at them with fascination.

The most impressive sight of all was the brontosaurus. Thankfully, another herbivore, the animal was over twenty-two meters long. Its legs looked like columns of concrete large enough to support a bridge. When it raised its head to eat leaves from a tree, it topped out near nine meters. The creature appeared to be slow, but so far Norz hadn't seen any potential predators. Even if T. rexes existed on this land, another dinosaur name he knew and could identify, he didn't think it could take down the brontosaurus. It seemed to him that the weight of one foot could crush the rex in one stomp. The tail was certainly large enough to knock a rex to the ground and possibly do more damage than that.

Norz imagined how this land could be turned into a zoo. People would flock from all over the world for a glimpse into times past. Why, once domesticated, dinosaurs might even be fed by hand and ridden. He saw himself as someone who, once they returned to civilization, would volunteer to return and work with others to make this dream a reality. This fantasy helped fill the hole he had in his heart since the dream of the Führer started to die. He could start a new life in a new world. Perhaps this new land would be a way to bring the people of the world together. Norz was tired of war, and the bitterness of defeat put things in perspective. He would be an international greeter here and take visitors on bus tours to the *ooos* and *ahhs* of travelers' delight.

Something crashed through the brush to their right side. It sounded larger than the small dinosaurs they were used to.

The five men spun on their heels and craned their necks as if to see past dense foliage, rifles at the ready.

A theropod burst through the tall grass and landed on top of Dorr, the last man in line. Dorr screamed as the beast raked its clawed feet across his chest. Before anyone could pull a trigger, it turned its head and hissed, and then leaped off and fled back into the cloak of the brush.

Marcks dropped to his knees and brought his hands near the wound, ready to help.

Dorr writhed in pain and pressed his hands against the cut.

The other three men surrounded the two, with rifles ready to fire.

"What was that?" Damzog said, the rifle barrel shaking from his trembling hands.

"I do not know—I do not know," Norz said. He was the leader, and it seemed he was supposed to have answers. He had been caught up in his own world and had let his guard down.

"That thing was as big as a man," Burhdorf said. "Did you see those teeth?"

"Dorr, move your hands and let me look," Marcks said.

Norz knew it was bad by the amount of blood pooling on the ground.

Dorr moved his hands and clenched them both into fists. He groaned through gritted teeth. The claw had sliced into chest muscle down to bone and poked a deep hole in his abdomen.

Marcks mumbled something to himself, his hand in the medical kit frantically searching. He came back with gauze and tape, and then proceeded to stop the bleeding.

Something sped through the brush again. Damzog fired blindly at it.

To the opposite side, something else was on the move. The three riflemen spun around, ready to fire.

Up ahead, in the clear open four meters away, a deinonychus charged toward them. Its two legs churned, clawed feet kicking up dirt, and its two short arms hovered by its chest. The eyes were ferociously aglow, and its mouth open, revealing backward-curved teeth.

Norz opened fire, uncertain of his target as it moved quickly before him.

A deinonychus leaped from the side brush, knocking Damzog to the ground. The beast clamped its jaws around his throat.

On the opposite side, another deinonychus sprang forth and took Burhdorf down. His screams announced his fate.

Marcks scrambled to his knees, picking up his gun, and hastily firing at Burhdorf's attacker.

Norz had fired eight rounds at the deinonychus by the time it leaped toward him for the kill. He didn't know how he was able to react so quickly, but he immediately fell to the ground and rolled. The back claw of one of the beast's feet narrowly missed him.

There was plenty of ammo left in his thirty-round magazine. Norz fired into the back of his attacker, hoping to hit a vital organ.

Marcks yelled in agony. All of the men were down. It was now one against three.

The dinosaur taking bullets swooned as it tried to turn and face him. It collapsed with its head crashing down, and he, again, had to roll to get out of the line of fire.

One down, two to go. Norz sprang to his feet and shot at the deinonychus feeding on Burhdorf.

The dinosaur let Marcks drop from the death grip of its jaws and charged.

Norz turned the rifle toward it and fired. The bullets packed enough punch to stop it in its tracks. He stopped shooting to conserve ammo.

Stealing a quick glance, Dorr had either died or was unconscious. Burhdorf was an unrecognizable chewed piece of meat. Damzog's throat had been torn out. Marcks' head had been crushed.

The two theropods lowered their bodies, weaving from side to side. Norz imagined they were sizing him up. Could they take him, or should they not press their luck and leave while they still could? They were wounded; bleeding holes in various parts of their bodies told that.

Norz didn't have many bullets left in the magazine. He weighed if he should take the opportunity to swap magazines now. Either choice was risky. There probably weren't enough bullets to take both of them down in the current magazine. Changing it out would leave him momentarily without defense.

The theropods' moves became more aggressive, and they started hissing a warning.

Norz took action to drive them back and buy a few spare seconds, squeezing the trigger, and alternating targets until the rifle clicked empty.

As soon as the bark of the rifle stopped, the two theropods charged.

He ejected the magazine and slapped at his hip, bringing up the spare. In it went at first try, and he pulled back on the bolt to load a bullet into the chamber. But even though he reacted in record time, it wasn't enough. The dinosaurs were on him in a flash before he was able to fire.

Norz's back hit the dirt. He felt the fiery brand of claws slicing away at his chest. A mouth opened wide, and rows of bloodstained teeth came toward his face. He smelled the stink of its hot breath as deadly spikes closed down on his head. Pressure rose in his brain until it felt like blood geyseried out his ears before the release of death took him on his final journey.

CHAPTER 15

A gunshot startled Commander Christoph Neuzetser awake. At first, he didn't know where he was. It was dark and his bed hard. Gone was the familiar curtain that separated his quarters from the command room. As sleep drifted, he realized he was sheltered in a cave. Sunlight cut into the darkness a couple of meters away.

A rifle repeated two more shots. He pushed himself off the thin blanket and headed out.

Crewmen sped to the direction of the gunfire, first stopping by the supply area to get rifles of their own.

The sunlight momentarily blinded him, and he had to wait a few seconds for his eyes to adjust. There was no immediate danger he could see. Crewmen were arming themselves for whatever may come their way. The fact he heard no returning gunfire made him believe they weren't under attack.

Klaus Barbie stepped out of the cave sheltering the Viktors, and asked, "Commander, what is the meaning of the gunfire?"

Christoph's mind was still clouded. He had expected to step out of the cave to the first soft rays of sunlight. Instead, he waded through bright rays of early morning. He looked at his watch and saw that it was 9 a.m.

"Commander?"

"I do not know," Christoph said. There was no use in saying anything that wasn't direct and honest.

"The Commander is supposed to be in charge, no?"

"I am in charge."

"You sleep all morning and you claim to be in command. No wonder we find ourselves lost in an unknown land."

The blood rose up Christoph's face. Barbie set a wedge in a crack, challenging his authority, and wasted no time prying it apart. "My men are trained to handle any situation, Mr. Barbie. That training was done under my command."

Crewmen bunched around one of the sentries as he came to the camp from guarding the perimeter. He held something bird-like by the throat, its tail dragging along the ground, and headed the commander's way.

The creature was another of those reptile/birds that were common. This one was about the size of a turkey. It had a reptilian head light blue in color. Its neck wasn't particularly long, and its brown, feathered crest matched its body. The wings were too short for it to take flight. Most noticeable were the claws on its hands and feet. The nails looked deadly enough to shred crocodile skin.

Bach followed alongside the crewman. Erik, wearing his backpack, meandered with others waiting for a better look.

Barbie wrinkled his nose and stepped back into the cave, where Dr. Mengele watched over the Viktors.

Stangl and Eichmann emerged from behind to join in examining the kill.

"Commander, this creature was stalking me. I tried throwing sticks at it to chase it away. It attacked me instead. It came at me and struck my leg." He pointed toward bloodstained trousers. "I stomped it off and managed to kick it away with my other foot. When it recovered and started to attack again, I shot it," the crewman said.

"I am confident you did what you had to do," Christoph said as he bent over and ran his finger over the creature's claws. "Find a place to put it, so others can have a look. Then, clean your wounds. I do not want your injury to become infected."

"If we had some liver dumplings, I believe the bones would make a good broth for a fine soup," Stangl said.

"Eh? You can have my portion," Eichmann said.

Both the SS officers went to the Viktors' cave when the crewman left to place the velociraptor on a fallen tree.

Christoph approached Bach. "Lieutenant, why did you not wake me this morning?"

Bach shrugged. "I did. You told me *in a few minutes*. I came back a half hour later and you were snoring. Frankly, I envied that you were able to sleep. There was nothing going on at the camp that needed your attention. I decided to look over things. If I needed you, you were just right here."

Christoph turned his gaze to the ground. "I do not remember you waking me at all." He rubbed his brow and carried his fingers across his face.

"It matters not. Get some coffee in you. You mind is fresher with the addition of sleep to handle the duties of the day," Bach said. "I will be taking a few men back to the U-boat for the remainder of supplies."

"Good. Carry on, Lieutenant," Christoph said. Their journey to camp included weapons and ammo, so some of the foodstuffs had been left behind.

Erik stood near the dead creature as two other crewmen pulled its wings aside and examined it.

Christoph approached his son, and asked, "Why are you wearing your backpack?"

"I am going with Lieutenant Bach back to the U-boat. We are going to bring the rest of the supplies back."

This brightened Christoph's mood. He had expected Erik to spend the day sulking about camp. "Did the Lieutenant ask you to help or did you volunteer?"

"I overheard him this morning, and I volunteered. I…I wanted to get away from camp," Erik said with hesitation in his voice. He stepped away and put some distance between the others.

Christoph followed without question, and then asked, "Tell me why you want to get away from camp? Are you trying to get away from me?"

"No…." Erik's gaze drifted downward. "The SS officers…I do not like them."

"Why? Did they say something to you?"

"No. It is a feeling I get when I'm around them. I…I do not trust them. I hear some of the crewmen talk…."

Christoph believed he understood now. The boy had heard the rumors about the officers not letting any of the other crew live after being rescued. "I am aware of the rumors." He looked again to make sure no one was in earshot. "Lieutenant Bach and I have discussed the matter. Erik, son," lowering his head, and gazing into his boy's eyes, Christoph said, "We have vowed that if we find such an arrangement has been made, we will terminate the possibility." Christoph watched Erik's expression to indicate if he understood.

Erik nodded slowly. His mouth tightened, and his eyes looked away as if imagining the scene. "Viktor is not who he says he is," he said in a whisper. "The SS officers hold secrets from you."

Before Christoph could inquire further, the rattle of a semi-automatic rifle cut through the camp. Erik's words pushed from Christoph's thoughts. "What now?"

*

Heyse and Bartels stood guard sixty meters from camp on the south side. Both men had been on alert since the three shots of rifle fire.

"What do you think happened?" Heyse asked. His left eye twitched as an unseen insect buzzed around it. He swatted the air in front of his face to shoo it away.

"Something, or *someone*, must have been a threat," Bartels said. "Americans?"

Bartels shrugged. "Unlikely. I would not think the American's would send only one scout out. Plus, there was no return fire."

"Some kind of animal, then?"

"It would not surprise me. Those things, like over there." Bartels pointed to a small theropod watching them from behind a low fern leaf, not three meters away. "And over there and there." His finger went to the left and then the right. "When we arrived yesterday, they were frightened of us. Most ran and hid as we passed. Now, look. They are bolder. We have invaded their land. Perhaps some are becoming brave enough to challenge us. Maybe they are wondering if we are good to eat."

"Eh, I would squash something that small with my boot," Heyse said. "I—"

Bartels watched Heyse's eyes widen like a shade springing open. "What?"

"A tree moved behind you!"

Bartels spun and saw a two-legged theropod as large as the trees as it emerged and charged their way.

*

A second rifle's bark joined the first as Christoph sped toward the supply area. "Erik, stay here. Get a weapon but do not follow."

The commander snatched up a *Sturmgewehr* and sped, along with the other crewmen, toward the gunfire. He quickly glanced back at Erik to ensure he had complied with his order.

Erik had frozen in place by the supply area. The sight was ironic, as Erik, with his black shoes and gray socks pulled tightly into place, his dark shorts, and *mud and camel* fabric shirt tucked neatly in, looked like any fine Hitler Youth waiting to serve his country. The pack on his back brought back an instant memory of sending his son off to school looking no different than he did at this moment. Such innocent times.

The blood-curdling death cry of a crewmate jerked him back into the emergency. Hearing a man's soul snuffed out was always unnerving. The roar from an unknown beast made his knees weak.

As Christoph composed himself, a second crewman succumbed to the same fate. As more rifles joined in, crewmen heading toward the fray now fled back toward camp in retreat.

"What is it?" Christoph asked as a crewman whizzed past.

"Monster!" The man kept his legs churning nonstop.

SSSHHHAAAGGGTTT! the beast thundered over the gunfire and terror-laced screams.

When the dinosaur came into view, Christoph braked to a stop without even thinking about it. His gaze lifted from the theropod's mighty legs up to its hideous jaws, where teeth clamped around a crewman's torso, as his arms and legs hung limply toward the earth. Was this a T. rex? The dinosaur was big but not as big as he had imagined. This one was either young or a species of theropod he wasn't aware of. Didn't matter. It was made of flesh and blood. He and his men had weapons and would fight back.

Christoph steadied his aim and fired at its chest. Small trickles of blood indicated that bullets had an effect but *were the projectiles deadly enough to kill it?*

Men backed away as the ire of the allosaurus increased. It flung the crewman in its mouth to the side and snapped at another who had turned and run.

Ten rounds from his gun in the beast, and no telling how many others rounds it had taken from others, had done nothing to slow it. The dinosaur's head constantly moved, so he had concentrated on targeting the chest where he thought the heart should be. Now, Christoph patiently waited for the head to move between his rifle's sights.

Bam! Bam! Bam!

His bullets ripped toward the allosaurus' head, at least one striking it in the left eye.

The dinosaur reared its head backward and uttered a deep, reptilian bray. It then leaned forward, turning its good eye in the direction of the blow.

Christoph darted behind a tree, thinking all he had done was make it madder.

The allosaurus stepped forward and jutted its neck toward the tree the commander hid behind.

The dinosaur's roar felt like a steam whistle blowing a scant meter from the other side of the tree. Christoph turned and ran. Large feet with railroad spike-like claws crashed down in hot pursuit.

The allosaurus roared again. The commander felt his body became weightless as if his feet no longer touched the ground. He didn't know how far ahead he was and didn't dare take a split-second to turn and look. Zigging and zagging, using the trees as best he could to slow its pursuit, he came to the presence of mind that he realized in his fear he had inadvertently led the dinosaur back to camp!

"Dive to the ground, Commander! Dive to the ground!" Bach yelled.

Christoph instantly recognized his lieutenant's voice and wasted no time in complying. The military had taught him in situations where seconds mattered that there was no time to question orders.

He hit the ground on his belly and slid across dry leaves. Placing his hands over his head, he closed his eyes and expected the worse.

One grenade exploded, and the allosaurus answered in obvious pain. Rifle fire continued, and two more grenades went off.

Boom! Boom!

Dirt and something wet rained on Christoph. Gunfire continued for a few seconds, and then faded.

"Commander, are you okay?" Bach asked.

Christoph flipped off his stomach and sat with his rear on the ground. The dinosaur laid on its side. One of its legs was nearly blown off by the grenades. Its chest looked like ground meat from all the bullet holes. A large hole cratered its stomach, more damage from explosives, entrails sloppily spilling along the ground.

"I am fine," Christoph said as he rose. He brushed dirt and bits of flesh from the top of his forearms, smearing the dinosaur's blood mixed in the mess. All he managed to do was transfer the muck from his arms onto his palms. Not wanting to wipe his hands on his clothing, he looked about for a large-leafed plant.

A low noise, similar to the buzz of insects, emerged in volume. As the sounds became louder and more distinct, there was no questioning it was from some type of those reptilian-like birds.

The brush came alive around them. A crewman screamed as a velociraptor attacked him from his blind side. The dinosaur looked just like the one killed earlier. It savagely ripped into his thigh and bit at his hands as he tried to pull it off.

More startled cries followed by gunfire coming from all directions told Christoph a full-scale attack had been launched.

Velociraptors invaded the campsite by the dozens. The fierce creatures were unintimidated by the humans or the discharge of gunfire.

Christoph grabbed for his sidearm and pointed the Luger at a raptor coming in for the kill. He waited for the dinosaur to get within a couple of meters before double tapping the trigger.

The velociraptor *hiss-cawed* as its legs weakened. Its momentum carried it forward, and it collapsed at Christoph's feet.

He considered his shots more luck than skill. Still, it wasn't difficult to kill these dinosaurs. The problem was hitting the targets before they got hold of their victims. Christoph watched in horror as the velociraptors teamed up on crewmen, biting and slashing as feet kicked and arms flayed. The raptors used the sickle-shaped claws on their second toes to tear at the soft flesh of throats.

Erik! Where was Erik? Christoph turned to locate his son, and a stray bullet whizzed by his ear. In the pandemonium, bullets flew in every direction.

He caught a glimpse of Erik standing behind Lt. Bach. Erik had a rifle up to his shoulder, but the bewildered expression on his face told he wasn't mentally prepared to fight.

Christoph ran to a crewman who had succumbed to the enemy. As the two velociraptors fed on the sailor's flesh, the commander peppered the bodies of the predators with the remaining bullets in the gun. Two more dead with many more to go. He ejected the pistol's magazine and jammed in a fresh one, ready to fight once again.

*

"What is all the shooting?" Adolf Hitler, the real man under the disguise of Frank Viktor, asked. His patience had been growing thinner by the minute in this confounded place. How did the commander manage to run a U-boat so far aground in the first place? Inexcusable! And now there was some level of attack. Had the Americans found them?

"I'm scared," Eva said, reaching out in the dim light filtering inside the cave and finding her husband's trembling hand.

"Doctor Mengele, give my wife another sedative," Hitler said. He gently squeezed Eva's fingers, feeling the tension growing in her grip. "There, there, my love. You have nothing to fear...you have nothing to fear." He wished he believed his own words.

Blondi's ears perked straight up, and her back began to bristle. She darted for the cave's entrance, where Klaus Barbie guarded, his pistol drawn.

"Creatures like the crewman killed earlier are attacking!" Barbie said. He raised his gun and fired two shots.

Hitler lifted his back off the blanket and sat upright, pulling his hand free from Eva. Gunfire, men's yells, and guttural caws from the bird-dinosaurs electrified the air. The madness reminded him of the last few days hiding in the bunker under the streets of Berlin. He and Eva had barely escaped with their lives their final day in Germany. There were no covert operations going on in this strange place to come and rescue them. *No! I must live. I will have victory over the Allies! I will shame them tenfold for what they have done to the Fatherland.*

Blondi's barks turned into snarls as she sped from the cave's entrance. A loud yelp followed, soon replace by whimpering cries.

The blast from Barbie's pistol amplified between the cave's walls as if striking blows against Hitler's head.

Then he saw one of the predators as it leaped toward Barbie's outstretched arm. It dug the claws on its feet near his wrist, and the gun dropped from his hand.

Barbie yelled and tried to beat the creature off with his left hand.

Mengele cowered to one side of the cave wall.

"Use your gun, you fool!" Hitler ordered Mengele.

Unsteadily, the doctor removed his weapon and cautiously stepped toward the entrance as Eva nervously cried.

Barbie's yells increased as more velociraptors took him to the ground and began the feeding frenzy.

Mengele fell backward at the onslaught of raptors entering the cave, his head falling a meter away from Hitler's feet. The doctor bellowed like a stuck pig—his voice strained with agony.

The first velociraptor to reach Hitler landed on his chest. Sharp claws pierced his skin, sending waves of pain throughout. Its toothy mouth snapped inches away as his raised arm shielded his head.

Eva screamed now, horrible shrieks sounding almost feline. Hitler felt her blood splattering on his arms and cheeks.

The velociraptor reached a claw toward his face, but the bandages on his face and neck kept it from slicing his throat. Then, both of his legs lit on fire, as more dinosaurs joined the fray.

The pain was unimaginable. Multiple claws cut deep, and flesh ripped out in chunks from the powerful jaws of the raptors. Each second felt like hours as teeth mutilated his arms while fighting them off.

His mind flashed to a report he read where his scientists put a man in a room of starving bedbugs to gauge how long he could survive. The man screamed and slapped at his body for over eight hours until he became exhausted, and then let them feed until his death. At this moment, he had an idea of what it was like to suffer like the commoners who fell to his whims. It seemed so wrong to die this way. No human deserved to suffer horrific pain such as this.

Jaws latched onto his nose. Cartilage cracked as a hungry velociraptor ripped it from his skull. Blood gushed down over his lips into his mouth, the metallic taste, bitter. Claws scraped along his scalp, streaming crimson down his head.

More claws dug into his abdomen. Hitler's pain was so great he no longer heard his own dying screams. His sphincter muscle loosened, and he soiled himself.

When will this end? He prayed to God to make the pain stop. To let him just die. To have the peace of void.

Then he thought of all the others who had suffered by his will. How none of them deserved such a horrible fate. For the first time, he felt guilt. No level of reasoning could absolve him from his sins against mankind, including the Gypsies, homosexuals, and *even the Jews*!

Hitler now saw himself differently. He was no longer the savior of his people. He had become Satan to the rest of the world, and in turn, became the destroyer of his beloved Fatherland. All the evil he had perpetrated combined to assign sins to his soul. How many? Thousands? Hundreds of thousands? No, *millions* of sins blackened his name.

A hum rose in his brain, pushing back on the pain riveting his body. At last! At last, death would arise to cradle him in its arms and take him away. The muscles in his back began to relax, and he had the urge to curl into the fetal position. He was becoming calm and felt like a child waiting for his mother to come in and tuck him in at night.

Then the faces of the innocent, those emaciated faces with eyes devoid of life appeared. The atrocities they had experienced by his hand carved into their expressions. They opened their mouths and began to cry, scream, plead with every ounce of energy for mercy. Others faces, young and old, of every race, creed, and color, lifted from broken bodies blown to pieces in the rubble of cities and the slaughter fields of war. A jury of spirits hurled accusations at the fallen leader.

Above the faces, a giant white throne appeared. From the dais, the Being of Light lifted its left hand and pointed.

Hitler looked as a massive lake of fire formed. Its surface boiled like molten steel as orange and blue flames licked toward the heavens.

Adolph Hitler felt his soul leave his body. The fiery lake drew him toward his final destination.

*

Eichmann and Stangl had engaged the allosaurus, along with the others, and now stood side-by-side targeting the velociraptors.

It surprised Eichmann that something that small in size could be so deadly. It further surprised him to see crewmen overwhelmed by the beasts and the ease of which they killed. So far, he and Stangl had held their ground, killing almost as many as shots fired from their rifles. By the looks of things, the tide appeared to be turning their way. As more raptors fell, the predators' tactics became less certain.

"To your left!" Stangl called out.

Eichmann stood between Stangl and a velociraptor charging from the side. He hastily squeezed off two rounds before the dinosaur leaped toward him. In one smooth move, he brought the butt of the rifle square against the raptor's chest. One of the animal's front claws extended enough to dig a groove out of his left wrist.

The velociraptor fell to its back and fluttered its wings, *hisscawing* in anger.

Stangl's rifle boomed by Eichmann's side. The bullet ended the threat.

"Good shooting, my friend," Eichmann said.

"Eh, I won a plaster Krampus at the carnival once for being such a marksman."

"The Führer!" Eichmann said the realization aloud. The two of them had been so caught up in the battle that neither had considered the safety of their leader.

With no immediate threat to delay, the two sped toward the caves.

Eichmann's heart sunk when he saw the dead body of Klaus Barbie and two raptors feeding on it. He put his arm out to slow Stangl, and then came to a stop, watching from ten meters away. Blondi lay dead not far, suffering a similar fate. From the sound of things, there were more velociraptors in the cave doing the same.

Eichmann looked over at Stangl.

Stangl shrugged and replaced the magazine in his rifle. "Looks like we made it back a bit late."

Dropping his magazine, Eichmann reloaded and raised the rifle. "I'll take the two on the left, you, the one on the right."

Five shots later, three more velociraptors lay dead.

"Let's go," Eichmann said.

The two stormed the cave and took out targets as they presented themselves. The cries from velociraptors reminded Eichmann of the time he fired a shotgun into a murder of crows.

When the dust and turmoil settled, Eichmann counted seven velociraptors dead in the cave.

Dr. Mengele's insides draped across his torso onto the ground.

Eva had a nasty cut deep into her throat.

Adolph Hitler's entire body looked like it had been painted in blood. Flesh had been stripped to the bone in places on his arms and his legs. Intestines and body goo adorned his thighs.

"Such a violent death," Eichmann said in a trailing voice of empathy.

"I've done worse," Stangl said. "Much worse."

Eichmann turned an icy gaze at his companion. The future was even more uncertain now than before. "The Führer is gone. The dream cannot continue."

"No matter. I can go back to owning a ranch and supervising gauchos. I will, however, personally do all the branding," Stangl said. "There is something invigorating about the smell of smoldering flesh." He walked over to Barbie's body, fished out a nearly empty pack of cigarettes from his pocket, careful to avoid unsavory body fluids. After tapping one free from the pack and placing it between his lips, he said, "Do you have a match?"

*

SKEER-AK!
Overhead two giant pterosaurs, like the one they saw on the beach when they had arrived, circled above. The smaller pterosaurs in the trees chattered at the carnage below. Some left the safety of branches to harvest the flesh of dead sailors and velociraptors strewn across the jungle floor.

Christoph now had a rifle and stood alongside Lt. Bach and Erik. Ironically, the tide of battle shifted from the predators to the prey as the velociraptors, distracted by their kills, paused to enjoy the spoils. Gruesomely, dead sailors became bait and the raptors easy targets. Crewmen giving a reprieve from being hunted avenged the lives of their fallen mates.

Erik had overcome fear's hold and fired sporadic carefully-aimed shots. Christoph didn't have time to know of his son's success and concentrated on watching for any hidden threat lurking to attack.

A human cry, not heard for several minutes, cut through the air.

Christoph and Bach turned and saw a new threat had invaded the camp.

One deinonychus had its mouth clamped on a crewman's right arm and another had the left arm down its throat to the elbow. The sailor's head jutted back as he screamed toward the heavens. The dinosaur with the left arm pulled its head back, stripping flesh to the bone. Blood squirted to the ground as if from a broken water pipe.

The shock of seeing the man-sized theropods had faded quickly. Christoph and Bach had their rifles up in an instant and ran toward the fray. Both had hesitated, not wanting to misfire and hit the crewman. With the fate of the man certain now, Christoph fired first, with Bach following after.

The theropods immediately loosened their hold. The sailor collapsed to the ground in a useless attempt to stop the bleeding of his left arm with his injured right hand.

Unfortunately, the commander and lieutenant had chosen the same target. While their combined gunfire sent the deinonychus in retreat, the ire of the other inspired it to charge.

Both only had time to squeeze off one shot before diving to either side as the theropod never slowed its pace and blew right past them.

With his right side on the ground, Christoph rolled over to see the deinonychus bounding toward Erik. "Run, Erik! Run!" he yelled, scrambling to his knees.

Erik started running well before the warning came from his father. The short distance between the dinosaur and the boy closed by the second.

Something blocked the sunlight from above as Christoph, left knee to the ground and the other leg up, propped his right elbow on his thigh to steady the rifle's aim. To shoot the dinosaur, he had to lead his target. If he overcompensated, he might hit Erik.

A shadow passed over him as the sunlight once again beamed down on his shoulders.

The theropod was too quick, and his nerves too unsteady, for him to fire a shot. An instant before the deinonychus lowered its head to grab the prey, taloned feet and huge bat-like wings swooped into Christoph's field of vision.

A giant pterosaur sunk its claws into Erik's backpack and lifted him into the air. The deinonychus' backward-curved teeth missed his son's boots as it sprung up to claim its prize.

Bach rushed to the commander's side and fired at the theropod.

Christoph stood, and with chin hanging, watched powerlessly as his son rose above the treetops and faded out of sight.

Gunfire rattled in greater numbers on the other side of the camp. Apparently, these accursed monsters hunted in packs.

Bach's bullets had either missed the deinonychus or it was so mad at losing the kill that it didn't matter if it had been hit. The dinosaur hissed and charged toward the two officers.

Their combined firepower inflicted enough pain for it to hesitate to a stop. A split-second later, it turned and ran for the cover of the jungle.

"Erik," Christoph said as his eyes gazed above the tree line.

"We'll find him, sir." Bach patted the commander's left shoulder.

The battle had ended on this side of the camp. The two officers of *U-616* sped toward the remaining threats.

*

Artur Phelps' boots pounded the jungle floor as he led his recon team back to basecamp. They had awoken with the dawn in hopes of arriving in time for a hot meal for lunch. Making camp before noon was a certainty now, as they were nearing the camp's eastern perimeter. Phelps was eager to deliver his report to the commander of the giant dinosaurs they had seen. He relished the opportunity to give a blow-by-blow detailed account of how they had witnessed the bloody battle between the triceratops and the T. rex.

Nearby gunfire from the camp told him that his crewmates more than likely had a story of dinosaurs to tell of their own. His main fear now was that there wouldn't be many left to tell it.

His mind raced with a T. rex terrorizing the camp. The huge beast stomping its way through, crushing men underfoot, and making snacks of puny humans. *Would bullets be enough to stop it*, he wondered. He wished for something the size of *U-616*'s deck gun and firing 8.8cm shells into the chest of the massive beast. At least he knew the men at the camp had a good stock of grenades.

Phelps was first to come upon a deinonychus feeding on a fallen crewman. The dinosaur was no larger than a man, but he instinctually knew it had more power than he and his four men combined. Thank goodness combat wouldn't be hand-to-hand. He lifted his *Sturmgewehr* and peppered the beast's right side.

The theropod sprang back, a piece of liver hanging from the side of its mouth.

As each sailor arrived by Phelps' side, they joined in on the shooting spree.

The deinonychus, under the onslaught of lead, turned to flee, but only managed to stumble a few feet to the ground.

This gave Phelps some confidence that modern firepower would give them a chance of survival in this strange land, and the realization they needed to get out of there before their ammunition ran out!

"What is that thing?" Ernst Ziegler asked.

"Maybe the smaller ones we see grow up to be this size," Wilhelm Lange said.

Roland Gwerder had rushed to the dead sailor's side. He ran his fingers along the victim's neck, and then examined the eyes. "He is dead."

"The hole in the chest told us that," Fritz Witt said. "We are wasting time. They need us at camp." Without waiting, Witt took off toward the nearby caves.

Phelps followed close on Witt's heels, the other three in tow. Dead sailors and dead bird-like dinosaurs along the way told the story that there was more than one type of enemy in this war. The small dinosaurs didn't look nearly as threatening as the larger one they had just disposed of, though he did notice the talons on their claws and feet. The amount of human carnage among dead, feathered carcasses indicated how lethal they were.

A human *yelp* from behind pulled Phelps' head around. A deinonychus' sneak attack picked off Ernst, who was the last in line. Before Phelps could react, Witt fired his rifle. Turning to see, a deinonychus stood in their path and headed their way.

By this time, Lange and Gwerder had opened fire on the dinosaur who had knocked Ernst to the ground. Phelps joined Witt in shooting at the frontal attack.

Bullets did nothing to deter the nasty beast. Their combined aim must have been off. Witt's *Sturmgewehr* steadily spit lead up to the point the deinonychus stuck out its neck and bit down on the stock, taking the sailor's left hand with it. Witt screamed and now stood between the dinosaur and Phelps, who was forced to hold his fire.

The deinonychus wrestled Witt to the ground, and with its backward-curved teeth, went for his throat.

Phelps heard Gwerder scream over the gunfire behind him. He didn't have time to look to see who was winning the war, but it sounded like the odds were against his team.

With the deinonychus' head within reach, Phelps lowered the rifle barrel directly against the creature's skull. He unloaded the six remaining bullets at point-blank range.

The dinosaur protested not. Its body went limp, and its head listed to the side. Bloody teeth stained with parts of Witt's throat wickedly smiled toward the sky.

Phelps looked down at the gaping hole and Witt's glassy eyes gazing into infinity.

Artur Phelps hadn't noticed the gunfire behind him had stopped until Lange put a hand on his shoulder. The leader jumped and went to bring his rifle up.

"It's me. Calm yourself," Lange said.

Phelps looked over at the two sailors and the dinosaur lying still on the ground. "They are dead?"

"Yes, unfortunately. From what I can tell, Ernst's neck was broken when the dinosaur knocked him to the ground. Ernst was always a fragile man. That is why I made him my friend, so I could care for him." Lange wiped a tear that trickled down his face, smearing dirt across his cheek. "Gwerder's gun jammed, and he attacked the dinosaur with the butt of his rifle. It was a foolish thing to do…I know he was only thinking of saving Ernst."

"They were good men. All, good men," Phelps said.

"The best," Lange's words faded. He then lifted his head after taking a deep breath. "We head to camp."

"We will come back and bury them," Phelps said.

"Yes, we will. And we will eat the flesh and drink the blood of the devils who had dared to attack us."

*

Christoph and Bach arrived at the side of Stangl and Eichmann in under a minute. By this time, gunfire had all but ceased. Of the crewmen forming a loose circle of defense, Christoph counted eight. *Eight!* This was impossible. Others had to be alive. Somewhere, hiding in the jungle waiting for the battle to end.

Perhaps they ran out of ammo. He felt the need to call out for everyone to come back to camp.

Then urgency in Christoph's mind relaxed and allowed his eyes to drink in the carnage strewn across the jungle floor. Dead carcasses of the bird-like dinosaurs littered the area, mixed with tens of bodies of his own crewmen. Of the larger theropods, like he and Bach had engaged, he counted four dead. From the looks of things, those dinosaurs had killed as many men as the dozens of smaller ones had.

"Commander!"

Christoph looked over and saw two crewmen approach. Hopefully, there would be more.

Phelps waved his hand in the air as he trotted forward.

Instantly, Christoph recognized Artur Phelps, the leader of one of the reconnaissance teams. With only one man with him, he assumed danger infested this whole accursed land.

The two men's faces showed disbelief as they scanned the campsite.

The commander walked over to greet them. "The others?"

"Commander, we were just outside of camp when we heard the gunfire. The group was whole, then. As we got closer, we saw we were late arriving to the battle. These...these two-legged dinosaurs, as big as men, attacked us. We killed two of them, but not before...not before they took three of us."

"I am sorry," Christoph said, seeing the weight of the men's fate on Phelps' sagging shoulders. "We have lost many men today."

"The other team...Norz, Dorr, Damzog, Marcks, and Burhdorf. Have any of them made it back?" Lange asked.

"No, not yet," Christoph said.

"What have you to report?" Eichmann said. He and Stangl had eased their way over next to the commander. "Did you find the Americans? How many are in their party?"

Phelps turned his gaze and held it there a second at where the T. rex-looking dinosaur lay dead. He then said to Eichmann, "We did not go very far to the south. Nowhere near the beach. We turned around just before dark to leave an area where a T. rex killed a triceratops. I thought it was too dangerous to risk the men with animals that large and us only having rifles to fight with."

"Are you sure it was a T. rex? Did it look like that one over there?" Christoph asked as he pointed at the dead creature.

"I only know a few dinosaurs by name. From what I can tell, the animal we saw was bigger than the one dead. Its head looked different, too. I would think the two are different species, but what do I know? I am just a bosun in the *Kriegsmarine*."

SKEER-AK! a giant pterosaur screeched from above.

Christoph stomped a couple of meters over, raised his rifle into the air, and fired until it clicked empty. He didn't know if he had hit the flying reptile or not, but at least he had scared it away from camp.

"Really, Commander, was that necessary? The ringing in my ears from the earlier incessant gunfire had all but gone," Stangl said.

"During the battle, a pterodactyl as big as that one picked up his son, Erik, and flew away," Bach said.

Christoph remained alone, staring at the sky, his rifle pointing to the ground.

"Such a tragedy. Perhaps Captain Christoph is no longer of sound mind to command?" Eichmann said.

"No one is taking my command from me," Christoph said, not bothering to address Eichmann face-to-face. Right now, any attempt to relieve him of duty would be met with a bullet meant to kill.

"Very well, Commander, what is the plan?" Eichmann asked, his question sounding of a veiled dare.

Raising the rifle across his chest, he turned and walked back to the others. "We go north. We need to get to a high point and get the best vantage of our surroundings."

"But what about *Erik*? Should we not go and look for him?" Bach asked.

Christoph dropped his head, and said, "I would say *yes* if I had a clue where he might have been taken. My heart tells me he is still alive, but my head says there is no way he has survived this long. A hungry, wild animal wastes no time..." he shut his eyes and swallowed dryly, "eating its kill."

Bach rested a hand on his commander's shoulders.

"I have a duty to the living," Christoph said, looking over at the ten crewmen who hung on his every word. "We need to leave this area now. We do not have time to bury our dead. The pterosaurs are already feeding, and other scavengers are sure to come. Everyone, gather all the essentials you can carry. I want to be on our way before a half hour ends."

Turning back to Eichmann and Stangl, Christoph said, "I take it Barbie, the doctor, and the Viktors did not survive the battle."

"No, the cave had all the décor of a slaughterhouse," Stangl said.

Christoph went to turn but hesitated. "Tell me, either of you. Who were this Frank Viktor and his wife?"

The two stared back like poker players making bets while holding winning hands.

Stangl finally said, "He was a simple man whose heart knew no boundary for the love of his country. He was a student of the fine arts, with opera and painting catching his fancy. Such a good soul was he that he refused sustenance from the flesh of animals, and at times gave graphic accounts of their butchery in an effort to make his dinner guests shun meat. He was a dreamer and believed that God in the heavens loved the Aryan race above all others. He was the lion and the wolf. But roses are planted where thorns grow. And as he cleansed his garden from the deadly barbs, the neighbors allowed the thorns to grow out of control, overwhelming everything in life he had worked so hard for." He stopped for a moment and gazed around his audience. "He was you, and he was me. We were the empire." Again he paused, and then said, "The empire is no more, and now the lion and wolf are deceased."

After a moment, Christoph said, "Good. Then our future is left up to us what to make of it." He turned to his crewmen. "Let's gather supplies and head out."

The men turned, including Eichmann and Stangl, and did as ordered. Bach remained by his side.

"If the SS officers did present a threat, I think with Viktor gone that is no longer the case," Bach said in a low voice.

"I agree," Christoph said. "I believe we will find Eichmann and Stangl more cooperative."

"Sir, please, let me go and search for Erik. You lead the men to the high point. I know chances for him are slim, but I can at least…at least bring you back some closure."

Christoph's lips curled into a sad smile. "I know you speak from your heart. But I need you now more than ever by my side. Come, Lieutenant, we must prepare for the journey, too."

He lowered his head and started for the supply area, his mind drifting back to the day Gerda brought home an infant set of lederhosen for Erik. The boy looked precious beyond words. And now, now he was gone.

Christoph swallowed back the bittersweet memories and wondered how long he could keep up the charade of leadership before falling to pieces.

CHAPTER 16

Erik, knees locked as he watched a crewman getting torn apart by two deadly dinosaurs of a type they had not seen before, sprinted for safety as one bolted from its victim and bowled past his father and Lt. Bach. The instant he took off running, he knew this would be a race impossible for him to win.

The theropod grunted at each step, and now, Erik practically felt the hot breath of the animal on his neck.

Something hit him dead-center in his back. He keeled forward, but instead of falling flat on his face, his shoulders jerked upward with such force that his feet quickly left the ground.

At first, he had wondered if he had died and if his soul was leaving Earth, soaring toward Heaven. Or perhaps an angel had come from above to fly him safely away. When the bat-like wings flapped to the side, gaining altitude, he realized his savior looked like something more from Hell than Heaven.

A giant pterodactyl, its wings over ten meters wide, had him by his backpack, and now carried him over the treetops. The camp was no longer in sight. There was jungle as far as the eye could see. No cities, no towns, nothing but pristine land untouched by the manipulating hand of man.

Erik was helpless in a situation that had no good ending. He could wiggle his arms enough to slip out of the backpack, but the fall was sure to kill him. If he waited until the flying reptile landed, he would be faced with nothing to defend himself with other than the 120mm blade of his Hitler Youth knife.

SKEER-AK!

The cry of another pterodactyl came from behind. Now there were two of these creatures he would have to deal with. Erik did not think the situation could get any worse, but it had.

Something crashed into the pterodactyl who had him in its grasp, and the world spun sideways as his captor rolled with the blow. The other pterodactyl had attacked, willing to battle for the prize.

Erik gagged from the turbulent motion. The reptilian funk wafting from the creature's body compounded the situation.

His captor didn't give up, speeding away over towering treetops, and heading toward a mountainous rock with a single strange looking tree growing out a distance from its base. It didn't take long for Erik to realize his final destination. The tree had a large nest near the top. In the nest two pterodactyl youths waited with eyes closed and hungry mouths open, anticipating their mother to bring them their next meal.

The other pterodactyl dove by without making contact this time. Erik's captor shrieked out a warning. There would be a fight for whose children would dine on the soft flesh of the human.

Erik pulled the knife from the sheet metal scabbard, its grip slightly worn from use at camp. One of his favorite games to play involved throwing the knife underhanded and embedding the blade in a tree. He had developed his skill enough that, from a certain distance, he almost always made a successful throw. There would be no tossing of the knife in this fight, and he had little confidence in his hand-to-hand battle skills.

The pterodactyl swooped down toward the nest and pulled up as it neared, flapping its wings as it momentarily hovered.

SKEER-AK! the challenger cried from above.

Erik felt the talons loosen from his backpack, and he fell two meters to the bottom of the nest.

The two hatchlings, anticipating their mother to feed them regurgitated bits of meat, would have to wait for her return. Their eyes had yet to open, but the two were nearly as big as Erik, and their long beaks with serrated teeth looked sharp.

The nest, at least, softened Erik's landing. His feet hit first, but then he fell forward to his knees. He maintained his grip on the knife and quickly sprang to his feet with his weapon poised to defend.

The pterodactyls were less than a meter away and sensed that something was in the nest with them.

One closed its mouth and leaned its head toward Erik, perhaps to locate food by smell.

Erik struck its beak with the flat side of his blade, hoping to discourage its curiosity. He saw a path of escape down the tree and onto the rock mountain, but his footing would have to be sure as the nest hung precariously from the mountain's side a good twenty meters in the air.

The battle between the mother pterodactyls blasted from overhead. If he didn't get out of this situation in a hurry, he would face a beast much worse than those that threatened him now.

The hatchling's head recoiled from the blow, but instead of giving up, it came in for an attack. It reached out its head and clamped down on Erik's left forearm.

Pain jolted through his body. Instinctually, he lashed out with the knife and stabbed the hatchling in the neck.

It squawked in high-pitched intensity. Surely, this cry would alert the mother that her precious children were in danger.

The hatchling's beak remained clamped around Erik's arm. He repeatedly pulled the bloody blade from the winged reptile's neck and stabbed in abandon.

Frantically, the hatchling flapped its wings, striking Erik on the side of the head. But the boy persevered, digging the blade deeper with each blow, and cutting furrows in its flesh.

Finally, the pressure on his arm subsided. Erik pulled it from the limp beak and pushed away from the slouching beast. It was dead. The other hatchling had not joined in the attack and still waited with an open mouth for its mother to feed it.

Erik's forearm felt bruised, and two shallow cuts on the upper and lower side were left from the imprint of the beak. In all, he was in relatively good shape and wasted no time sheathing his knife and climbing off the nest.

The tree was a little too large for him to wrap his arms completely around it. So, his descent slowed with caution. At least the trunk grew from the mountain at an angle, and he didn't have to travel straight down. One meter at a time, his heart pounding, the war cries of the flying reptiles *cheering* him on, at last his feet hit *terra firma*.

The rock mountain offered no place to hide. He maneuvered as quickly as possible the sixty meters or so down the rocky surface to the flat ground below.

As he dashed toward the dense jungle, he realized that the whole time he went down the mountain, he had not heard the cries of the battling pterodactyls. A bad feeling washed over him. The back of his neck felt hot, and his cheeks felt tingly.

SKEER-AK!

The screech sounded right by his ear! Something hit him in the back, and he plowed face-first to the ground.

The winning pterodactyl landed two meters from him, coming to claim its prize.

Erik flipped over and rose on his knees. He frantically slapped at his side to pull the knife from the scabbard! But it was too late. The reptile's triangular-shaped head jutted forward. Its pointed beak opened wide as it came in for the death blow.

Bam! Bam! Bam!

SKEER-AK!

Erik fell to his side and lifted his arms over his face.

Bam! Bam!

It wasn't until the second volley of gunfire that Erik realized someone was shooting.

AK-AHHAK! The pterodactyl, wounded, pounded the air under its wings until it gracelessly became airborne and fled.

Erik felt the air kicked up from its hasty departure. Unbelievably, he had been saved!

He rolled to his side and saw a figure approach. It was an American sailor, his rifle pointed at him, his finger on the trigger.

***

Adam Rodrigue traveled briefly by the gulley after narrowly escaping the hungry jaws of troodons, uninspired by his chosen path. He at least knew heading west would lead him to the ocean, but how far away from camp he would be, he didn't know. To make matters worse, a dinosaur bigger than a double-decker bus, with a duckbill and a strange horn-like thing growing backward on its head, veered him from his path. The problem compounded as he tried to travel back west with other dinosaurs, some who had walked on all fours, and some with bird-like characteristics, and inadvertently pushed his path north.

He at least had enough sense not travel far in the wrong direction. He elected to take refuge in a tall tree before dusk and spend the night, and stay there for the morning, unable to make a decision of what to do.

It was possible Captain Brazo would send out a rescue team for him. Even if that happened, the chances of them actually finding him seemed almost zero.

Just as he left the tree, deciding to head south and taking his chances crossing the tree bridge over the gully, risking the possibility of facing more troodons, he heard shrieks coming from the nearby rock mountain.

He was shocked when he saw a boy, who looked to be in his early teens, choose his steps carefully as he navigated the side of the mountain to the ground. He was even more shocked when he saw a giant pterodactyl leave the heavens and career toward him.

Adam pulled the wad of gum from his mouth, stuck it behind his ear, and double-timed it over toward the boy. Just when the creature knocked him to the ground, Adam stopped and fired his M1.

The pterodactyl's leathery body presented a huge enough target, though from where Adam stood, he couldn't tell if his bullets found the wing or the beast's body. No matter, his shots were sure enough to send the animal scurrying back to the skies. The boy narrowly escaping death by mere seconds.

With the threat gone, Adam cautiously approached the boy. He realized that no more than two or three years separated them in age, and he had no visible weapon. That said, there was always the possibility he might have a grenade. The boy had a backpack, and there was no telling what was inside.

"Are you okay?" Adam asked as he steadily walked forward.

The youth rose to his feet and brushed off his pants, never taking his eyes off Adam's.

"I said *are you okay*?" Adam had spoken louder and with an edge in his voice. It was obvious by the boy's clothing that he was a member of Hitler's youth. The Germans *had* made it to shore, as Captain Brazo suspected.

The youth's right hand drifted toward something on his right hip. It was a knife.

"I wouldn't do that if I were you," Adam warned.

The youth's hand froze in place.

"You gotta name?" Adam asked.

"*Sprichst du Deutsch?*"

"Don't play with me, boy. I know all you Germans over there speak French and English. Plus, you understood enough not to go for your knife."

The youth remained still, his eyes showing no recognition.

"Aw, come on. I just saved your life. You can at least talk to me. I ain't gonna shoot you unless you do something stupid."

Biting his lower lip, the youth reached over with his right hand and gently touched the cuts from the hatchling's beak on his left forearm.

"Hey, you're bleeding. You hurt?"

The youth nodded his head.

Adam turned his gaze all around, and then up at the sky. "Look, I don't like standing out here in the open. Seen too many dinosaur things. I ain't gonna leave you here alone. What say you that we call a truce and try to help each other? I got some stuff in a pack that I can clean your cuts with."

"Erik, my name is *Erik*."

"Eric, that's an American name," Adam said.

"My name in English is spelled with a K on the end and not a C."

"Yeah, you Krauts use different letters in your names than we do. I remember thinking that when I read some news stories."

"What is your name?" Erik asked.

"Me, my name's Adam. Like the first man, *Adam*. You know about *Adam and Eve*, don't you?"

Erik shrugged. "I am Catholic."

"What? No way! I'm Catholic," Adam said. It dawned on him that he had just assumed that the Germans, because of all their evil ways, didn't believe in God.

"My mother was Catholic, and I am Catholic, too. Germany has many Christian citizens."

"Well, if we're both Christian nations, why are we fighting each other?" Adam wondered aloud, internally questioning how two countries believing in the same God could be at such odds.

Erik shrugged again. "I guess the war is not about religion."

That answer sounded as logical as any, Adam guessed. Still, they were wasting more time, and he was ready to go back and take cover under the trees. "Okay, I'm going to lower my rifle. We have a truce, right? I promise I won't do anything to hurt you, and you keep that knife in that scabbard? Deal?"

"I agree to a truce," Erik said.

"What's in the backpack? You ain't got no weapons in there, do you?"

"All I have is a canteen. The backpack is empty because I was on my way to fill it with supplies when our camp was attack—" Erik's eyes widened as if he realized he let out more information than he thought he should.

With his rifle pointed to the ground, Adam said, "Com'on over here. Let's walk under the shade of that tree over there." He waited for Erik to step by his side, and then matched strides with him by Erik's right side, keeping a furtive watch on the knife.

Once under the tree, Adam asked, "So, what cut you? Your arm's sliced top and bottom." He had Erik's wrist in one hand and ran his fingers near the cuts. "Not too deep. Blade must have been kinda dull. Not really a clean cut."

"I was bitten by a flying reptile—like the one you shot. It was much smaller, though, a baby."

Adam chuckled. "I was going to say *if you got bit by one as big as I banged up, you wouldn't have an arm*." He let go of Erik's wrist and pulled a medical pouch on his side. Retrieving a cotton ball and a small bottle of rubbing alcohol, he opened the bottle, and put some on the cotton. "Now, this may sting a bit." Adam chuckled again. "You know what, I sound like my mom. Your mom ever tell you that when she puts an *anti-septic* on a cut?"

Erik smiled for the first time and nodded. Abruptly, the expression fell from his face.

"Hey, what's the matter? Am I hurting you?"

Erik sighed. "No, it only hurts a little. My mother did say those words to me when she cared for my wounds."

"Well, I guess mothers are the same all over the world," Adam said.

"I guess you are right," Erik said, lowering his head. "My mother was killed in the war."

Adam's heart sunk with the weight of Erik's words. It was obvious the memory was fresh and there had been little time for the grief to pass. "Aw, I'm sorry, man. That's tough you lost your mother." Just as quickly as his compassion rose for Erik, he remembered his Uncle David, and how his loss still affected him. It reminded him of his hate for the Germans who had killed his uncle. A hate that he couldn't transfer toward Erik at this moment for some reason.

"You know, when you get right down to it, war just don't make no sense. People just need to learn how to get along. All this fighting and dying just ain't necessary," Adam said, mainly to himself. He tossed the crimson-stained cotton ball aside and pulled out a bandage roll from the med-pack. Adam began wrapping Erik's arm.

"Adam, I have been thinking the same thing. War hurts every side in the fight. We are better off to find ways to be friends and not enemies."

"Well, we have a truce. Soon, the war in Europe will be over, anyway. There's no reason to keep fighting. The Allies won. You Germans are just gonna have to deal with it, just like losing the first world war," Adam said, trying to sound like he wasn't boasting.

Erik lowered his head and gazed at the ground.

The poor kid had lost his mother, got separated from his people in this place, and his country had no future after taking half the world on and losing. Adam put himself in Erik's shoes and knew how low the boy must feel. "Say, are you hungry? I know I am."

"Not very. I had biscuits and fish earlier this morning."

"I didn't eat last night. I could use some grub." Adam reached behind his ear and unstuck the wad of gum he had put there minutes ago. "All I've had since yesterday is this gum. You want some gum? I got another piece."

Erik nodded.

Adam reached into his pocket and pulled out a stick of Dentyne chewing gum. "It may have got a little wet yesterday, but the wrapper's still on it."

Taking the slightly-mashed stick of gum, Erik carefully peeled off the paper and popped it in his mouth. "*Danke.*"

"Yeah, *dahn-keh*," Adam said, thinking the word either meant *thanks* or *good gum*. "I got two peppermints I was saving in case I couldn't find nothing to eat." He looked around, and said, "Okay, so, before I saw you I had decided to try and make it back to camp the way I came. Thing is, I know how to get most of the way there, at least to this big gully where I only know one place where we can cross. After that, I was at least going to head west and find the ocean, and then try and find where we landed. There were these two-legged dinosaurs, not quite as tall as you, that chased me from camp. If they're still there, I don't have enough ammo to kill them all."

"Would you take me to my camp?" Erik asked.

"I...*don't think I like that idea*," Adam said. After a long pause, he said, "How far is your camp?"

"I do not know. The flying creature held onto my backpack and lifted me away to here. I am not sure how far or in what direction."

"If I asked how many of you are at your camp, would you tell me?"

Considering the question for a moment, Erik said, "Would you tell me how many are in your camp if I asked you?"

Adam almost reminded Erik that he was the one with the gun but thought better. "You'll find out sooner or later, *if* we make it back to camp." In an attempt to clear the slight tension brewing, he said, "Okay. Let's focus on getting out of here alive. If we make it back to my camp, you can meet with Captain Brazo. You can decide what you want to tell him. The captain is a fair man. He won't let anybody hurt you."

Erik looked at Adam, with defeat in his eyes, and slowly nodded.

"You'll be okay. I promise. And we Catholics always keep our promise, right?"

Nodding again, Erik's expression brightened.

CHAPTER 17

Adam and Erik had come upon a dinosaur about the size of a large German Shepherd guarding a nest loaded with big eggs.

The dinosaur had long legs that kept its beefy chest well above the ground and an unusually large head. Its face and nose looked like a wide, flat beak. At the top of its head, bone jutted out, reminding Adam of the Pope's hat, in a silly sort of way.

The dinosaur appeared docile, grazing on vegetation while guarding its nest. Adam had decided to try and steal some eggs by deceit rather than force.

Some twenty feet away, Erik peeked from behind a tree.

Adam had left him there and ran a half-circle to flank the protoceratops. Getting as close as he dared, he gave Erik the signal, a simple wave of the hand.

Erik tossed a rock several feet into the brush near the protoceratops.

The creature, muted brown and green in color, stopped eating and lifted its head in the direction of the threat. It turned its head from side to side but didn't move from its watch.

Adam waved again, and another rock crashed into the brush.

This time, the protoceratops' eyes locked toward the noise, and it trotted off to find the interloper.

Carefully avoiding foliage that might crunch beneath his boots, Adam lightly stepped to the nest. These eggs were larger than a chicken's; *nearly eight inches*! He grabbed the front edge of his shirt and created a makeshift basket, fighting to maintain the rifle hanging from its strap on his shoulder. Keeping his eyes in the direction the mother dinosaur had exited, he placed six eggs in his shirt before hearing her make her approach back. Time for him to leave, no need to be greedy.

The eggs jostled about in his shirt as he took long, slow steps, aiming not to do anything to attract attention. He and Erik had agreed to rendezvous back at a particular tree whether his task had been successful or not.

Adam had been the first to arrive and knelt by the tree's large roots. He removed one egg at a time from his shirt. These eggs weren't hard like chicken eggs. Instead, the shell gave a bit, like they were made from leather. He had no idea if dinosaur eggs were fit to eat, but he was hungry enough to give it a try.

Gazing around, he saw no sign of Erik. Had the boy decided to take his chances on his own? Emptiness hit him in the stomach, and not from hunger. Adam had only met the boy over an hour ago. The two didn't really have that much to say to each other, but just having him by his side made Adam feel better.

Then he caught a glimpse of Erik as he rounded a tree. His eyes went wide in surprise when he saw the German boy's knife in his hand.

He removed the rifle from his shoulder and leaned it against a tree root. If he needed to, he could have it up and in his hands in an instant.

Erik caught sight of him and waved, placing the knife back in the sheath. The boy hurried his pace.

Tension left Adam's back, and he waved in return.

"I see you were successful," Erik said as he approached. He gingerly stepped over tree roots, choosing one high enough to sit on comfortably.

"Yeah, did you see the size of these eggs? Man, I bet it would take three or four chicken eggs to equal one of these."

"Are we going to eat now?"

"You bet we are. I just hope dinosaur eggs taste like bird eggs," Adam said, sat down, and then picked up an egg and pushed a fingernail into the shell. "These shells aren't hard. You ever ate a duck egg? I love duck eggs. The yoke's bigger than in a chicken egg."

"No, I do not believe I have ever eaten a duck egg."

"Well, they're the best. Except if the ducks have been eating crawfish. Then the eggs taste kinda nasty because crawfish eat dead stuff." Adam watched Erik's head tilt to the side. "You know what a crawfish is, don't you?" He set the egg back with the others. "You know, it's a crustacean. About this long." He held fingers from each hand a few inches apart. "And has claws." He held his hands out, separating his ring and index fingers in a claw-like fashion.

"*Hummer?*" Erik said, holding fingers from either hand a foot or more apart.

"No, crawfish don't get that big. I bet you're thinking of lobster. Well, think of a crawfish like a *little lobster*."

Erik nodded. "How will we cook the eggs?"

"I was thinking about eating them raw. Sounds gross, but some people eat raw eggs. I got some matches. We can build a fire and try to cook them in the shell."

Twigs snapped from behind Adam.

Erik lifted his gaze, and his jaw dropped.

***

Captain Brazo stared down at the sailor's innocent face as he placed the Colt .45 back in its holster. Gone was any contortion from his expression of fear induced by the ferocious dinosaurs who so savagely attacked. The bullet left a hole in the sailor's skull the size of a half-dollar: a window to crimson-gray jelly.

The remaining crew of eighteen softly approached, many with collapsible shovels, and all with freshly loaded rifles. Under the soft sounds of an unthreatening jungle, the wind lazily shaking leaves in the trees, and an occasional cry from the indigenous bird-creatures, the crewmen set to task at burying their shipmates.

No one spoke a word to the captain. Even Executive Officer Slick gave him his space as he dealt with the personal sacrifice of ending the suffering sailor's life through a violent act of mercy.

Brazo heard shovels hit dried foliage and dig into the dirt. He slowly turned and stepped out of the way so the crewmen could offer the last gift to their fallen brothers. Leaning against a tree, he rubbed his sweaty forearm across his brow, smearing dirt and grime.

This place was as deadly as any front in Europe or the Pacific. The dinosaurs were only flesh and blood, though, not manmade hulking masses designed with the only purpose to kill and destroy. Still, their predatory nature made them the most formidable foes. The men who had survived only did so by the slight advantage given by modern weapons. Weapons that were viable only until the last bullet casing spit out its crown of lead.

Lifting his shoulders, and straightening his back, Brazo boldly turned around and gazed over the scene, steeling himself to the harsh reality in an effort to strengthen his resolve as the leader and ensuring confidence in his command of the men remaining in his crew.

XO Slick caught his gaze and raised a hand in salute. Brazo returned the gesture, solidifying the bond of command, loyalty, and the heartfelt friendship.

The land permitted shallow furrows, willing to receive the dead souls who moistened its dirt with blood. Within an hour, the bodies were laid carefully to rest and covered with the blanket of foreign soil. No time was taken to mark the graves. Nothing in this land would acknowledge proper respect.

Brazo gathered his men by the rows of graves. Standing before them, he started from his left and slowly looked each individually in the eyes, sharing the window to his soul and looking through theirs. The last and eighteenth face he looked at was Jim Stone's.

Stone's expression weighed with sorrow but showed no sign of defeat. There was a gleam in his eyes that said he saw something in the situation beyond what he could see, touch, taste, hear, and smell. He had breached the paradigm of the three-dimensional world and saw with eyes above mortal man. Brazo had a feeling that if he were to pull Stone aside and ask him to explain, that no words in the human language could adequately convey the staunch faith that inspired such a unique man. A faith Brazo thought he would never care to have. A faith, though, that appeased his curiosity now unlike any other time in his life.

His hands behind his back, Captain Brazo said, "Our fallen brothers are gone but not forgotten. Each died protecting us, giving us the gift of life. This is a gift that must not be squandered. The burden on us is to carry on until we find a way off this place. We owe them that. They will live with us in our memories until the day we die."

Someone sniffed loudly and several more sailors cleared their throats.

Brazo continued, his voice loud and clear, "I was that which others did not want to be. I went where others feared to go, and did what others failed to do. I have seen the face of terror, felt the stinging cold of fear. I have cried, pained and hoped. But most of all, I have lived times others would say were best forgotten. At least someday, I will be able to say that I was proud of what I was, a seaman." Brazo raised his hand in salute, returned by the crew, and said, "We wish you Godspeed." He lowered his hand to his side.

Jim Stone lifted his gaze to the heavens, and said, "The Lord is my Pilot, I shall not drift. He guides me across the dark waters. He steers me in deep channels. He keeps my log. He pilots me by the star of holiness for His name's sake. Yea, though I sail 'mid the fenders and tempests of life, I shall dread no danger for He is near me. His love and care shelter me. He prepares a harbor before me in the homeland of eternity. He anoints the waves with oil, my ship rides calmly. Surely, sunlight and starlight shall favor me on my voyages, and I will rest in the Port of our Lord forever."

It didn't bother Brazo in the least that Stone spoke from his heart. He momentarily considered asking the crew if anyone else would like to say a word, share a memory, to shed some of the built-up grief. But, there was no time for that. The battle with the dinosaurs had caused enough commotion that had surely been heard miles away. The smell of dead meat festering in the jungle sun would soon have the nose of the carrion eaters. It was time to leave and find a safe place before dark.

"Men, it's time we gather what we can and head north," Brazo said. He saw uncertainty on his crew's faces, their minds probing the unknown. "Are you with me?" he asked.

"Sir, yes, sir!" the men said, responding to their training, and stiffening to attention.

"Executive Officer, Slick!" Brazo called.

"Okay, men. Let's pack up and get ready to leave." Slick led the short hike back to the supplies.

*

The remaining crew of the *USS Sutton*, walking five-wide, side-by-side, slowed to a halt as they reached the camp's perimeter. Brazo continued forward as the men parted, seeing two clumps on the ground surrounded by the small theropods and a few pterosaurs. There were two dead dinosaurs like the ones who had attacked them earlier also, not far from the clumps. Strangely, nothing fed on the dinosaurs' carcasses.

Hampton Wallace and XO Slick joined Brazo to either side as the captain sure-stepped toward the dead bodies of his crewmen.

The flying reptiles, these the size of hawks, took to the air in fear. Something long and stringy swung like a pendulum under the beak of the last one to leave the ground.

The small theropods ate greedily, some giving occasional hisses to companions encroaching their territory. None seemed concerned with the three humans walking toward them.

Brazo's boot met the underside of a theropod's tail, punting the little devil over the first body stripped of most of its flesh, and sending the other feeding theropods scattering.

Wallace fast-stepped over to the other body on the ground. The closest theropod looked at him as he launched his boot toward it. It darted out of the way just in time and hissed. "I'll get ya!" He swung his boot wildly, trying to make a connection, only to send the creature fleeing for the safety of the jungle.

"You want some of this?" Wallace said to the eight or so theropods surrounding the body, stomping the ground as he approached.

The theropods got the message and all scattered before feeling the brunt of a leather boot.

Whitish, red-stained bones basked under the soft orange of the approaching evening. Brazo had seen his share of dead men in his career, some injured in the most gruesome of ways. These two men resembled skeletons on display at a Halloween carnival. All the flesh had been eaten from the faces, and the eye sockets gazed emptily toward the heavens. Eerily, their hair still covered the tops of their heads. Seeing a smiling skull with hair sent chills up his spine.

After a shallow breath, Brazo reached down and jerked the chain and dog tag from what was left of Danny Underwood.

Wallace didn't wait for orders and removed Joey Gridley's ID.

Jim Stone approached and took the dog tags from each, placing them in a bag on his side filled with the IDs of others who had died earlier.

"See that dinosaur over there?" Wallace said, pointing. "I think Rodrigue managed to kill it and run away. If you look at the brush, you can kinda see a path."

Brazo walked over toward the dinosaur, with Slick following him. He looked at the ground, and said, "I see his footprints. He made a run for it, all right."

"Yeah, and the other footprints tell us that more of these monsters went after him," Slick said, disappointment, but not surprise, in his voice.

"At this point, he headed north. We'll follow the path as long as it stays in that direction. If he's alive, we might get lucky and find him," Brazo said, his words sounding hollow in his own ears. *Luck* is not what they needed. They needed *intervention*. At this point, he began to think the unthinkable. Beggars couldn't be choosers. His fear of coming upon the Germans and going into an all-out war gave way to a new way of thinking. Could they form an alliance? Maybe, but only if they had been as decimated in this cursed place as them. If the Germans greatly outnumbered them, then all bets were probably off. Still, Brazo left his mind open. He needed to keep his men alive and get them out of here. At this point, the captain wasn't too proud to pray to God, nor was he self-righteous enough not to make a deal with the Devil.

*

Brazo's crew made temporary camp not long after an hour's march from the original basecamp. The cloak of darkness shadowed everything below the treetops, so making ground during the night was far too risky. The heavens above, though, sparkled with thousands and thousands of diamonds that looked like they had been collected in a jug and spilled across the sky. The captain had seen the night sky from the middle of oceans, far away from land. He had never seen the intensity of majestic beauty as this night had brought. For the first time, he understood why the ancients had deemed the galaxy the *Milky Way*.

With only eighteen left in the group, Brazo had insisted on pulling guard duty along with the enlisted men. His shift began at 4 a.m., and he had surprisingly caught a few hours of sleep beforehand. He had been probably more mentally exhausted than physically tired. When he had laid his head on a thin, rolled up blanket, his eyes closed, and his mind shut down like a light switch thrown in the *off* position. Slick told him that he started snoring almost immediately. And, that the XO didn't know if his snores were more likely to attract dangers or scare them away. Brazo smiled thinking about that. Alan Slick had a knack of knowing simple things to say to make him feel human and not a killing war machine the US Navy had created.

The glow of dawn eased like an eraser on the eastern horizon, fading darkness with its orange light, and slowly transforming it into day-blue. The stars dimmed, too. Wisps of thin white clouds trailed upon their morning journey across the sky.

It was a new day, and with new days should come new hope. Brazo had to instill the hope in his men if they were going to survive.

"Well, at least we had a quiet night," Slick said, catching the captain in his thoughts.

"Yep. We all needed a break. Did you sleep well?" Brazo asked.

"Well enough. My legs are good for another day's march."

"Funny thing about mountains. They always look much closer than what they really are," Brazo said, glancing north.

"Well, where I come from, that thing is not big enough to be called a mountain. How long do you think it might take us to get there?"

"Terrain is uncertain, and you know how the jungle slows you down. Discounting being attacked, I say if we keep steady at it, we can reach the base by nightfall."

Slick rubbed the back of his neck. "Hmm, that's pushing it, I think."

"Well, I did say that high point looked closer than it probably is. I, at least, want the men to have an objective they will try to meet. If I'm going to lead, I'm going to *lead* big."

"Yes, you're right. That's what we're paid to do." Slick chuckled.

A crewman who had been relieved from his guard post walked up to the XO and captain. "Sir, I have a report."

"Go ahead, Sanders. Did you see something?" Brazo asked.

"About fifty yards from here, there's a gully as far as I can see in either direction, cutting through the path north," Bill Sanders said.

"A gully? How wide?" Slick asked.

"Dunno for sure. Ten, twenty feet. I couldn't tell how deep it is because I didn't go down there. Right now, we're on high ground. The land drops off maybe a hundred feet before it flattens out by the gully."

"Doesn't sound like this trip is getting any easier," Slick said.

"Well, there's a dead tree laying across the gully about a third of a mile west. It's a nice size tree big enough to walk on. We might be able to cross there," Sanders said.

Brazo's dim eyes brightened. "Okay. Good job, Sanders. If there's a way across this thing, we're going to find it."

"I'll give the orders for the men to get some chow in them before we move out," Slick said to the captain.

"All right. I want us out of here and by the gully in less than an hour," Brazo said.

"Yes, sir," Slick said and set off to spin the wheels into motion.

*

After a breakfast of hard biscuits, pemmican, chocolate tablets, and black water passed off as coffee, the team of Americans hiked north and down by the gully.

Footprints told the story that one human had come this way, along with a few dinosaurs. From the looks of the animal tracks, it was of the same variety that had attacked the camp. There were some blood drops staining the ground on top of the dinosaur tracks. Hopefully, meaning it came from them and not the human.

Brazo felt sure these were Adam Rodrigue's footprints. Yesterday, from their hike from basecamp to the new camp, they had traveled Rodrigue's path for a short distance until the boy veered off to the east. They did come to one point later where it looked like he had headed back north for a ways, but then went west. The captain assumed the crewman kept an erratic pattern to throw off his pursuers, still maintaining a northern trek, though.

It wasn't until the first man walked across the tree bridge and over to the other side that they knew Adam had made it that far. The ground showed only the imprints of his boots and not clawed feet of deadly dinosaurs. The boot prints basically went west from there, which was disappointing. Brazo couldn't afford to send men after him.

The depth of the gully was hard to determine because of the uneven edges and darkness. The angle of the sun needed to be directly overhead for them to get a better idea, although a rock tossed down into the middle of the abyss in places took a good ten seconds to return a sound.

The gulley was not an issue. Everyone had made it safely across the tree bridge, and the journey northward continued.

CHAPTER 18

Wilhelm Lange had insisted on leading the survivors of *U-616* to the commander's new destination. The nine other remaining crewmen offered no protest. Artur Phelps appeared to be relieved that the responsibility would not rest upon his shoulders.

Lange boasted that the hatred in his heart for these nasty creatures invoked the spirit of *Hermóðr*, an ancient Norse God, the war-spirit and messenger of the Gods. The energy churning within him would act as a repellant for any of the dinosaurs who might lurk along the way.

Lieutenant Bach watched the crewmen's gazes lock on Lange as he went on his rant. The man offered something that gave them hope and inspiration. At a time like this, faith in leadership was the most important component to survival.

The entire time Lange lobbied for leadership, Commander Christoph stared blankly toward the air in front of his face. Bach had no way of knowing if he was listening. The fate of his son was most certainly pushing all other thoughts from his mind.

Eichmann and Stangl had acted like the notion of one of them being first in line was well beneath their honorary stature. Both would turn and gauge Christoph's reactions at times as Lange's address rivaled the Führer's speeches himself. Disdain steadily crept across their expressions as Lange rambled on.

When Lange finally cooled down, spittle had frothed to one corner of his lips.

All eyes then turned to Christoph, who acted no more present than before.

"The commander has talents I was not aware of," Eichmann said. "He sleeps with his eyes open."

Christoph turned his attention to Eichmann, narrowing his gaze sharp enough to cut steel.

Before any sparks flew, Bach said, "The commander indicated to me to put Lange in front. He is a warrior at heart and will alert us to dangers we are certain to encounter."

Though Christoph never uttered a word, the energy emanating from him was such that defused any berating Eichmann and Stangl might have offered.

All of that had occurred a few hours ago. The trek through the jungle had gone surprisingly without incident since then. Bach wondered if all the gunfire and explosions earlier had scared some of the threats away. He didn't have faith in Lange's claim to God-gifted blessings. Deep inside, he kept waiting for their luck to fail and the pits of Hell to unleash the demons of this accursed land.

The lieutenant followed two steps behind the commander, keeping a wary eye for obstacles which might offer danger as Christoph robotically followed the loose line. Bach noticed the commander looked pale. Sweat continually rolled down his face and glistened under the hot sun. His cheeks sagged, and his face looked like it had aged twenty years. Christoph sighed deeply every few minutes, which apparently annoyed Eichmann. The elite SS officer would glance back at each sigh, his mouth and nose drew in as if he smelled something disgusting.

The jungle thinned a bit, and the terrain rose. The path north led to a high point in the area that, in reality, should have been thought of as a high hill. Climbing to the top would not be an issue. Getting there alive was the challenge.

Christoph sighed loudly, air rushing from his lungs like a bellows stoking a fire.

Eichmann, who was in front of Stangl, who was in front of the commander, stopped cold in his tracks. The officer spun on his heels, raised a finger toward Christoph, and said, "Enough! You sad excuse for a *Kriegsmarine* commander. You mope like a child, whereas, you should steel your resolve and be the man you were trained to be. Death is part of life. Those that live bury the dead and move on. You are not fit to command!"

The whole group had come to an abrupt halt. The two crewmen behind Bach stepped to his side. The rest of the group in front of the commander remained where they were. The time had come. For most of the trip, the SS officers had itched to take command. Christoph not only looked like he had lost his will to fight, but the will to live, also.

Bach knew better than to intervene. Stepping in for Christoph would do the commander no favors. Part of Bach worried this standoff would do more to lessen the group's chance of survival than facing another attack from a dinosaur.

The commander's blank stare toward the ground between him and Eichmann never wavered. He took the tongue lashing like a scolded dog.

"It is *you* who are responsible for bringing us here," Eichmann continued. "Your ineptness has taken the lives of most of your crew. You are not fit to lead sheep! I am relieving you of your command and will give the orders now." His hand shook as rage grew in his voice, his face and chest reddening, peppered with white splotches. "Say something, you spineless worm!"

Christoph weakly lifted his gaze. In practically one smooth motion, his right hand went down to his sidearm. The Luger snapped up, the barrel leveling with Eichmann's forehead. The crackle of a 9mm bullet discharging from the chamber sliced the tense moment in half. A hole the size of one Reichspfennig coin appeared between the SS agent's eyes, sending his head backward, and his body following it to the ground a second later.

With the gun still in hand, pointing at a body no longer there, the commander shifted his gaze over to Stangl.

The air stilled and time stopped. Seemingly, no one dared to breathe.

Stangl wiped the corner of his mouth and cleared his throat. He slowly reached down and carefully pulled a pack of cigarettes from the fallen officer's pocket. Before tapping one from the pack, he said, "You may put your weapon away, Commander Christoph Neuzetser. Apparently, our dear Eichmann misjudged you. Of which, I am sure, he wholeheartedly regrets at this moment."

Though everyone showed shock over the event, Bach felt like he was the one taken most off-guard. Something had shifted in the commander's psyche. Bach was close enough to the man to know he would not have reacted this drastically before Erik was taken by the pterosaur. This was a desperate time. People make desperate choices when options are few.

The brush and trees near the front of the line rolled and shook like a great wind blew past.

Lange, in the lead, had been captivated by the events of the last few minutes, just as all the others. As he turned and raised his rifle toward the disturbance, a dinosaur burst from the foliage.

The beast towered more than twice as tall as a man. It stood upright on two thick legs and had a long neck with a snake-like head. Though it looked similar to the huge beast that had attacked the camp, this creature had an array of feathers that ran from the top of its head, down its spine, and all the way to its thin and relatively short tail.

With lightning speed, the therizinosaurus' right arm carried an oversized hand with straight claws over a meter long into Lange's chest. The brave warrior managed sporadic fire while impaled by the beast's hand, the claws so deep the pointed ends jutted from his back.

The dinosaur roared in anger and struck quickly to end the life of its prey, bringing its head down, and crushing Lange's skull with its powerful jaws until it disappeared. Blood gushed up from the stub of his neck like an artesian well.

Of all the dinosaurs they had encountered, this one looked the deadliest. It had features of a T. rex and the fierce turkey-sized dinosaurs combined.

The surprise of the attack held everyone immobile for the first few seconds. Bach was the first to raise his rifle and fire. The others quickly joined in the defense.

The dinosaur shrieked, sounding like two rusty ship hulls scraping together. It flung Lange aside as if he were a ragdoll and charged forward.

The next crewman in line became in immediate danger and had little time to backpedal before its head snaked over on its long neck, and bit down on one of his shoulders. The man yelled like a newly castrated pig as the dinosaur lifted him off the ground and slung him into a nearby tree.

Bullets poked bleeding holes in the dinosaur's pale green chest but did nothing to slow it at this point. The men scattered for their lives as it advanced, claws slashing the air before it, and its head swiveling in search of its next victim.

The commander, though, had stood his ground. His rifle was on his shoulder, and he steadily pumped lead into the oncoming beast. A brave action, for sure, but Bach saw this as a death wish come true more than a heroic response.

In mere seconds, the dinosaur would be on top of the commander. Bach couldn't stand idle and let this happen. Tossing his rifle aside, he sprinted toward Christoph.

The dinosaur roared again as its head shot like a missile toward its next target.

The commander steadily fired as if he were in no danger whatsoever.

Bach crashed into Christoph, sending them both to the ground. The dinosaur's mouth clamped down on mostly empty air. One of its teeth, though, had managed to scrape the commander's left forearm.

EEERRRAAAPPPHHH! the beast screamed in frustration.

Not waiting for the dinosaur to take advantage of two easy targets, Bach sprang to his feet, helped Christoph up, and pushed him over to a fallen tree for refuge.

The tree was huge and situated in a way, amongst the large branches, to offer semi-shelter. Neither Bach or Christoph had their rifles to join in on the firefight. The thought of using their sidearms was blatantly ridiculous.

Another crewman's death scream announced the battle was far from over.

Christoph tried to leave the hiding place, but Bach held him firmly in check. "Commander, wait. I have a plan."

Christoph looked like he was going to protest but held his words.

Just as another man cried in pain, Bach emerged from the tree's cover, standing on a branch. The dinosaur immediately turned its head his way.

"Over here! Come over here!" the Lieutenant yelled while waving his hands.

Faster than he anticipated, the beast bounded toward him. He barely had time to pull the grenade from his belt, set the charge, and be in the position to toss it as the dinosaur's mouth gaped open to eat him.

The grenade left Bach's hand at the last possible fraction of a second before he bailed from the tree branch. "Get down! Cover your head!" he said, pulling the commander to the ground with him. The tree trunk should protect them, but if the dinosaur's head lingered above, shrapnel had a chance to get them both past the branches.

The grenade exploded. A few seconds later, something heavy thudded against the earth.

Bach scrambled through the tree limbs to get a look. All rifle fire had ceased by this point. The body of the therizinosaurus looked more massive than five bull elephants. The grenade had been effective. Its bottom jaw had become unhinged and a bloody mess. Apparently, shrapnel had found its brain.

Christoph had emerged from behind the tree and ran over to the nearest crewman, who stepped from the cover of the brush toward the dinosaur.

Bach made his climb over branches to join them.

Artur Phelps and another crewman took the gory task of examining the four-presumed dead. As expected, they would no longer have to endure the dangers of this accursed land.

The survivors eventually gathered near the head of the therizinosaurus.

"Look at that thing. It doesn't even look real," a crewman said. He reached his finger toward one of its glassy eyes.

"Leave it alone," Christoph said.

"Our fortunes are running low, Commander. With Eichmann gone, and the four crewmen dead, we now total nine in number," Stangl said. The man spoke as casually as if commenting on a difficult football match.

"We may be down to nine men, but my orders stand equally as well for one as a thousand. I will take the lead," Christoph said, scratching his left forearm. "I do not know what will happen over the next few hours, as each coming minute is a mystery. Let me just say now, in case I do not have the opportunity in the future, that it has been an honor to serve with each of you in the *Kriegsmarine*." He directed his attention to Stangl, and said, "Mr. Stangl, I honor your service to the Fatherland."

Stangl shrugged his shoulders. "If I would have been born British, I would have bad teeth and been a confidant of Churchill. You take life too seriously, Commander."

Christoph's head listed to the side. After a few seconds of silence, he said. "Mr. Stangl, you are correct. I do take life seriously." The Luger came up from its holster. Bullet met brain inside of Stangl's skull.

None of the men flinched at the discharge of the weapon.

Stangl had made no attempt to dodge the attack, an indifferent expression held tightly on his face.

"The remaining eight of us *will* take life seriously," Christoph said. "Gather what we need from our fallen brothers. Let us leave and face the future together." Christoph scratched at his arm again. The wound was now red and swollen.

CHAPTER 19

Adam Rodrigue saw fear grow on Erik Neuzetser's young face. The snapping of twigs behind him altered that he had failed to keep his guard up. His hunger had shadowed possible immediate dangers. Now, he might suffer his shortcomings by dying with an empty stomach.

His rifle resting within reach on a tree root, Adam sprang from his seat and snatched up his weapon. He spun around, expecting to see a reptilian behemoth with huge jaws and sharp teeth.

"Adam! It's me, Wallace!" Hampton Wallace said, the barrel of his rifle and his head poking from the brush.

Rodrigue's heart swelled. "Wallace! I can't believe it's you!"

"It's me, all right. The rest of the crew is right behind me."

"The rest of the crew? All of you came to look for me?" Adam asked.

Wallace chuckled. "Naw, it didn't happen that way." He lowered his head and his rifle barrel to the ground. "We got attacked yesterday. You know...I found Underwood." His gaze returned to Adam. "And, uh...yeah. It was bad. Those dinosaurs came at us, and it was a blood bath. I've never seen anything like it—never imagined anything like that could ever happen. I don't know how, but we managed to survive. Some of us, that is."

Adam thought of the dinosaurs that he fought off and escaped. They were tough but not unstoppable. "I knew things would be bad. I managed to kill a couple, so I was hoping our guns would be enough to save the crew."

"Yeah, the dinosaurs bleed just like any other wild animal. They're, they're just different than anything we've grown up with," Wallace said. He shifted his gaze to Erik. "I see you've made a friend."

Erik had remained seated with his knees together and his hands placed on top of one another in his lap. His eyes wide and his mouth tight, it was obvious the boy was scared.

"That ain't no friend of ours." Emerging from behind Wallace, Bob Brown stepped from the brush and into the open. "That's a stinking Kraut."

Brown was a gunner on the *Sutton*. Adam recognized the man, but really knew nothing about him.

"He's just a kid. He's okay," Adam said, taking a step toward Brown.

"You know what they say. *The only good Kraut is a dead Kraut*," Brown said, his words slow and threatening.

"Stand down, sailor," Captain Brazo said as he and the others exited the brush and gathered by the tree. All eyes were on Erik.

Adam watched the men, most looking like they had been in the worst fight of their lives and lost. Expecting to see a larger number, he asked, "Are more coming?"

"I'm afraid not, Rodrigue," Brazo said. "We lost over half the remaining crew yesterday before dark. I decided to take us north to a high point. There's no way we can hope to survive where we are now. Ammo is getting low, and our food won't last much longer."

"So, you found me by accident," Adam said.

"Yeah, though we did find your footprints by the tree bridge and knew you at least made it that far," Brazo said.

"You sure are lucky," Wallace said.

"I don't know about luck. Saint Valerie watches over me." Adam pulled the chain with the medal from under his shirt and displayed it across his chest.

"Saint Valerie didn't do the rest of the crewmen much good," Brown said. "Ain't gonna do that Kraut over there much good, either."

Another layer of tension fell over the situation. Adam knew if they ever made it back to camp there might be problems, but Erik was just a boy. He hadn't killed anyone. He believed what he believed because he was taught by others. There was no way of holding someone his age responsible for what his country had done.

"Rodrigue, who is this? Where did you find him?" Brazo asked.

XO Slick stepped over to Brazo's side.

Jim Stone meandered his way over near Erik.

"It was unbelievable. I had spent the night in a tree after dinosaurs had scared me in the opposite direction that I wanted to go. I thought about waiting for a search party to find me but decided to make it back to camp. That's when I saw this boy come running down a rock hill. He was being chased by one of those flying dinosaurs. You know, the great big ones that kinda look like a bat. Anyway, I ran over to help and managed to get a few shots off at that dinosaur before it got him. His name is Erik, Erik Neuzetser."

"Really? My name is *Rudolf the Red Nose Reindeer*," Brown said.

"No one asked you, Brown," Slick said.

Brazo stepped closer to Erik. "You do speak English."

Erik nodded. "Yes, I speak English." His gaze locked on the captain's.

"Tell me how you got here," Brazo said.

"I am not sure how we got here," Erik said.

"Erik, this is not an interrogation. We know that you were on the U-boat. The U-boat that put two torpedoes in my ship. I'm going to be truthful to you. I know you have no reason to trust me, but I am asking for your trust. I will be honest with you if you will be honest with me. Our countries are at war, but that won't last for long. Hitler is dead, and Germany is going to fall to the Allies. I promise I will do nothing to hurt you, or the others from the U-boat, if you will promise me the same," Brazo said.

"You're negotiating with a kid?" Brown sarcastically asked.

"You're going to be negotiating with my fist if you don't pipe-down," Jim Stone said.

"One more outburst from you and you'll do ninety days in the brig when we get back," Brazo said.

Brown looked like he was about to spout off a rebuttal, but XO Slick stuck his nose in the man's face. The crewman's insubordination melted, and he turned his gaze to the ground.

"Erik, tell me something. We're not hiding anything from you. You can count how many of us are left alive," Brazo said.

The young boy looked a little more relaxed. He said, "We were escaping Germany. Yes, we do realize that the war is lost. We meant no harm to anyone. I was in the command room when the Destroyer spotted us and came in for an attack. The commander had no choice but to defend the U-boat."

"Where were you going?" Brazo asked.

"I am not certain. Somewhere to start a new life."

"And here. Did anything happen inside the U-boat that might tell us how we got here?"

"I heard there was a storm. Electrical interference disabled the U-boat. We ran aground and were forced to make camp."

"Can you tell me where your camp is?"

Erik shrugged his shoulders. "I was taken from camp by a giant flying reptile. I lost all sense of direction. Adam found me as I escaped from the reptile's nest. He and I have made a truce."

"We know that there're around fifty people that can fit in a U-boat. Can you tell me how many are in your camp?"

Erik turned his gaze to the ground and sighed. "No, I cannot. We were under attack by dinosaurs when I was snatched away. I do not know how many are alive. I do not know *who* is left alive," he said, his voice breaking in the end. A small tear trickled down his left cheek.

"You had family aboard the U-boat?" Brazo asked.

Nodding in silence, more tears flowed down Erik's cheeks.

"Well, let's hope they made it okay," Brazo said and stepped away, giving the boy some space. Addressing the men, he said, "We've delayed long enough. Let's get going."

"Hey, can I have something to eat? I'm starved," Adam said.

"Here you go, champ." Wallace pulled a ration pack from a pouch and handed it to him.

Jim Stone turned to Erik. "Would you like something to eat?" He offered the boy one of his ration packs. "There's plenty to go around."

Sniffing back the tears, Erik shook his head.

"You sure?" Stone asked.

"Not now."

Adam avoided the tree's roots and went by Erik's side. He reached in his pocket and came up with a peppermint, handing it to the boy.

Erik offered a half-smile and took the candy. He unwrapped the peppermint and put it in his mouth.

***

"Commander, we should stop and make camp here. You are not looking well," Bach said as he trailed behind Christoph.

"There is an hour of light, and we are too close to the base of the high point to stop. We must get to higher ground and find shelter before it gets too dark."

Bach knew Christoph was right. Even at this pace, they would be in the position to make the ascent within a half hour.

Sweat saturated the back of the commander's shirt. Bach had made it a point to hand him a canteen every fifteen minutes so he would stay hydrated. The angry wound on Christoph's forearm crusted with a blackish scab, and a red streak ran up his arm.

Looking behind him, Bach saw Artur Phelps and the five other crewmen methodically keep pace. It was obvious they were going through the motions. There was little hope higher ground would do nothing more than cement the dire situation they now endured. What then? Struggle to live another hour only to know ultimately the odds would turn against them, and then die a horrible death being eaten alive? For the first time, Bach considered suicide a viable choice.

RRRTTTHHH...RRRTTTHHH.

The commander's hand went up, and the group held fast in their tracks.

Trees and brush were thick in the area. The noise sounded like a high-pitched growl, different from the jungle noises they had become accustomed to. How far away, Bach couldn't be sure.

After a good minute had passed, Christoph started moving again, his rifle up by his chest at the ready.

Bach's peripheral caught movement. He looked and saw a theropod slinking five meters to the east. From the distance, the size of it didn't look threatening. As near as he could estimate, it wasn't more than three meters long and only one meter high. Its body shape reminded him of a long-legged swan, because of its long, thin neck and narrow head. For a moment he considered firing off a shot, hoping to scare it away. Sometimes the best defense was a strong offense. But he realized that a gunshot might call attention from dangers far worse. Still, he didn't like the idea of that dinosaur slinking on the sideline.

RRRTTTHHH…RRRTTTHHH.

There it was again. Coming from a different direction this time and perhaps sounding closer.

Christoph stopped and motioned for the others to come to him.

When Bach arrived, he said to the commander, "Over there." He nodded his head to the side. "I do not know if that noise is coming from a dinosaur like that."

"There are two dinosaurs over there," Christoph said.

"Three…four…five," Phelps added as more gathered in view.

"Perhaps these hunt in packs, too," Bach said. "What do we do?"

"I wish we had a wall at our back," Christoph said, scanning the area. "They are gathering to attack. We must stand ready."

No sooner than the words left his lips, a coelophysis led the charge straight for the crewmen. Others poured from the brush, many hidden by the foliage.

Phelps was the first to fire. His aim, less than certain. The targets were fast, and their body size presented the minimum opportunity for a deadly hit.

Blood plummeted from Bach's face toward a growing pit in his stomach. A swarm of dinosaurs in this number would be impossible to survive. This was it, the last stand. Only for a brief moment did he consider pulling his sidearm and putting it to his head. Instead, he lifted his rifle and shot the first beast in his sight. It hit chest-first along the ground, its long neck twisting, and skidded to a halt.

More bullets made connections as dinosaurs shrieked in pain and others stumbled to the ground. The gunfire had managed to put hesitation in the onslaught, but a cry from a crewman, who had drifted away from the group, told he was the first to fall victim.

Bach saw that two dinosaurs had paired in the attack. One pulled on his arm, sending the man to a knee. The other had its long, narrow mouth clamped vise-like on the back of the man's neck.

Gunfire erupted in the distance. Some number of dinosaurs, who lingered in the attack, scattered in every direction, some headed toward the gunfire.

The situation was so electrified Bach didn't have the luxury to question who was coming to their aid. The lieutenant concentrated on a few dinosaurs, who stopped two meters away, and snaked their heads and open mouths toward the commander. He suspected the loud discharge from their rifles put caution in their attack.

All weren't so fortunate, as two more screams signaled the end of more lives.

The gunfire from behind the dinosaurs grew closer. Bach now saw the deep blue uniforms worn by the US Navy. The Americans had come to their rescue. Surely, they knew who they were fighting to save. An errant thought had Bach wondering if the sailors would stop with the dinosaurs and then continue until the Germans were eliminated, too. No time to be concerned with that now. Each second had to be won in order for the next second to have consequence.

A coelophysis charged the commander, sending him to his backside, and his head glanced off a stone the size of a dinner plate.

Bach unloaded his rifle into the dinosaur's side, keeling it over before its head could strike the commander. Another three charged for the kill. He quickly dropped the magazine and pulled back on the bolt, loading a bullet, and letting lead fly. He was sure he hit his targets, but their momentum carried them forward. One managed to hit him and knock him down, but he was on his feet in a flash, firing as even more charged forward.

The Americans had killed or scattered the majority of the dinosaurs between the two armies and closed the distance between them. But more than two dozen relentlessly attacked Bach and his crewmen.

Phelps' rifle clicked empty after dropping a dinosaur at his feet. The beast behind it struck with mouth open toward him, only to swerve at the last moment to avoid the bayonet on the rifle's barrel.

With the remaining dinosaurs clustered about the five survivors of the U-boat, the Americans only fired sporadically, obviously out of concern of hitting them.

With a rebel yell, an American charged the dinosaur challenging Phelps. The bayonet from his rifle penetrated the dinosaur from its backside and sunk in with a dull *thunk*.

The beast raised its head and brayed with pain.

Phelps dug his feet into the ground and charged forward. His blade found the dinosaur's heart. The deadly creature's body went limp, its head flopping over to the side.

For a brief second Bach saw the two opposing warriors stand side-by-side, ready to fight any onslaught.

But as his spirits brightened with the aid of the Americans, fire blazed from his left shoulder as a coelophysis' mouth clamped tightly. Teeth ripped into flesh, and the creature pulled him off balance to the ground.

The blue sky loomed overhead and white clouds blew wistfully by. A long neck carried a narrow head plunging from above. It happened so fast, Bach was completely at the situation's mercy. Though the battle neared the end, with victory for them and their new allies, fate had dealt him a death card.

The dinosaur's open mouth came down on Bach's soft throat. He felt the blood pressure rise in his head like it was a squeezed balloon. Warm wetness trickled over his neck and between his shoulder blades. His lungs could no longer pull in the precious air surrounding his face. Reality started to lose color. Dark blotches exploded like fireworks in his field of vision. The gift of life had run its course. Lieutenant Gunter Bach, for all the good and all the bad he had done in life in for but a mere dot on the timeline of human history, felt his soul slowly evaporate from his body. Peace rolled in, filling the void, and with peace, satisfying joy until oblivion.

CHAPTER 20

Though they hadn't spent two full days in this land out of time, the scene was all but too familiar. Dinosaurs ripped by modern weapons lay dead, strewn among the greatest treasure nations had to offer. A sacrifice for the freedom of others, so that few might preserve the wellbeing of the many. Sadly, despite their valiant sacrifices, now the many had become the few.

Captain T.W. Brazo watched the German boy, Erik, kneel next to a U-boat officer.

The only other member of the German Navy to survive, a man named Phelps, looked sadly about. Bags swelled under his eyes. His face was smeared with sweat and grime.

The connection between the German officer and the boy was obvious. Erik had to be his son. The facial features were uncannily similar.

To everyone's shock, the downed officer moaned.

"Father!" Erik said in surprise. Apparently, he had feared the worst, too. The boy placed his hand on his father's cheek.

The officer's eyes fluttered open. Weakly, he said, "Erik?"

"Yes. I am here," he said assuringly.

"*Aber*...." his words trailed, but his voice had brightened. Looking around, he became aware that he was no longer only in the presence of his companions.

"I'm Captain T.W. Brazo. I am...was the captain of the *USS Sutton*," Brazo said. "My men and I came to your rescue. You are in no danger, but I ask that you keep all communications in English." Brazo had already made the request to Phelps and the boy.

"Erik!" the officer said and pulled his son to his chest, with one arm. He closed his eyes and smiled. "I thought that I had lost you."

"I am fine, Father," the boy said.

The officer's eyes widened. "Phelps…my men…Bach!"

"The others did not survive," Phelps said.

Joy melted from the officer's face. Bitterly, he tightened his lips.

"Are you the commander?" Brazo took a shot at guessing the man's rank. He at least had more markings on his uniform than another officer who lay dead with his throat torn out.

"Yes. I am the commander of *U-616*. My name is *Christoph Neuzetser*."

"I'd be lying if I said *I was glad to meet you*. What I will say is that I am happy that you and your son are back together," Brazo said.

"I never thought I would see my son again," Christoph said, his arm still tightly around Erik. "How did you…?"

"It is an unbelievable story, Father. The creature who stole me away put me in its nest. I managed to escape, and an American sailor saved me. The captain rescued us. He and the rest of the Americans have treated me well. Many gave their lives fighting the dinosaurs attacking you," Erik said.

"Yeah. I lost twelve more men. There's no way we'll survive any more attacks of this magnitude," Brazo said.

"I am grateful for your act of kindness, and you have my sympathies for your lost men. It appears we have found ourselves in the same proverbial boat," Christoph said.

"That we do," Brazo said.

XO Alan Slick stuck by Brazo's side. Jim Stone had one eye on Phelps, who still had his rifle, obviously ready to move into action had the German made a threatening move. Adam Rodrigue and Hampton Wallace remained on watching the perimeter, along with the other two crewmen who had survived, Bob Brown and Bill Sanders.

Brazo looked about, and said, "I wish we had time to bury our dead, but we don't. My objective was to make it as close to the top of that high point before dark. We can't stay here any longer."

"That was our objective, too, before we were attacked," Christoph said. "We think alike, Commander."

"We wouldn't be commanders of ships in our nations' service if we didn't," Brazo said, ironically thinking of how the two *were* probably so much alike, only separated by the color of their uniforms and the belief of who was right and who was wrong. "How's your head? Are you able to travel?"

Christoph gingerly touched the left side of his forehead. "It is bruised, but I am able to travel," Christoph said.

"That wound on your arm looks bad," Slick said. "Better let me clean it up."

"It is but a scratch and of no concern. We must leave now, as the captain said. We must find safety for the night," Christoph said.

"Okay, let's once again go through the gruesome tasks of relieving our fallen men of food and ammo, and then we'll hike our way up the high point," Brazo said. "Commander, you and Phelps are only to attend to your men, as we will ours. Out of respect, of course."

"Thank you, Captain. You are most gracious. I cannot truthfully say I would have afforded you the same consideration if the circumstances were reversed," Christoph said.

Well, at least the German commander was being honest. Brazo had no way of knowing if he was making the right decision or not by letting the Germans join his team as equals. But his gut told him that with the odds in their favor, and the wellbeing of the commander's son a prime objective, there would be no meaningful conflicts between the two sides. At the first indication of trouble, Brazo had already discussed with Slick, who covertly passed it on to the others, they were to shoot to kill any attempted insurrection. Erik, the boy, would be treated no differently than any other man in the deadly game of war.

*

Tired legs and heavy hearts had trodden up the rocky incline leading up to the highest point in the visible area. The pace had been slow and steady. As the sun made its dip toward the horizon, the heat of the day dissipated enough to encourage all to push forward.

Commander Christoph, his son Erik, and Phelps pioneered the way.

Brazo and his six crewmen followed. The captain kept his eye closely on Christoph. Not out of fear of what the German officer might do, but more out of concern for the man's health. The commander's face looked gaunt, sickly, and he refused to rest more than five minutes at impromptu breaks.

The cloudless night and bright full moon allowed them to trek under the stars for a while. Fortunately, the terrain didn't offer many obstacles or any desirable shelters for dinosaurs to hide. There were a few varieties of pterosaurs, but nothing with a wingspan of over six feet. Brazo had wondered why some dinosaur hadn't adapted to this mountainous ground as goats had in modern times. Perhaps food was plentiful enough on the ground below. Still, he thought some of the weaker creatures might find safety on higher ground. At this point, he now feared something hiding in a subterranean cave somewhere might surprise them in the night. From all they had been through, why should their luck change now?

Luck? Were he and the six other Americans actually lucky to be left alive? Maybe the lucky ones were the ones who had died, but dying negated life. And life, life was the only real possession that ultimately mattered.

Brazo realized fatigue had affected his reasoning, sending circular patterns of doubt through his mind. Doubt that might lead to the deaths of them all.

With the distance to the top of the high point appearing to be within sight, there was no real advantage to advance that far. They had come upon a limestone formation with a smooth side, perfect to set up camp next to. No one protested when he gave the order.

Rodrigue took first watch as the others spread thin blankets to lie on. The campfire had matured into glowing orange-yellow embers, and they heated water in metal cups. The Germans shared rations of canned fish, passed on any of the American pemmican, but gladly took the chocolate offered to them.

Erik had spent his full attention attending to his father. The commander said few words, and the only food he ate was at his son's insistence. Jim Stone said Christoph had a burning fever, despite all the aspirin administered to him.

With food in the belly and hot coffee to the lips, tension released like dry, rotting bands on a rubber ball. Just when Brazo assumed everyone would soon drift away in their own thoughts and into the cradling arms of sleep, E-3 Bob Brown felt the need to stimulate conversation.

"What do you Jerries think is going to happen to y'all after the war?" Brown's mocking tone anticipated the worst of consequences.

Christoph might as well have been on the other side of the Earth and made no indication that he heard the American sailor.

Erik briefly glanced Brown's way, but then turned his eyes toward the fire.

Phelps cocked his head to one side, rubbing the thumb and pointer finger on his right hand together. "I imagine that like our situation now, we will be at the mercy of the Allies."

A smile swelled across Brown's gritty face. "Yep, imagine so. You boys shoulda learned your lesson after the first world war."

"I was but a child when that war ended. We could argue why Germany went to war then, but I have no expectation that you would understand any other perspective than the victors' view of history," Phelps said. "You see, the German people accepted their punishment and went to great lengths in fulfilling the impossible demands of the Treaty of Versailles. The monetary penalty heaped upon the German people, a country crippled by war and the loss of millions of working-aged men, was more than even the most robust of economies could bear. Most of my early life, I lived each day with gnawing pains of hunger. It took years for the Fatherland to heal and rebuild itself. If conditions had not been so harsh, perhaps our leaders would not have had the need to create a war machine to preserve our survival."

XO Slick snapped to attention. "Survival? Having a military to protect your country is one thing. Invading other countries and conquering them, quite another."

"You speak of imaginary lines on lands thousands of years old. Search your history. Those lines have been redrawn multiple times over the generations. Austria welcomed their annexation in nineteen thirty-eight. There was a German majority in Sudetenland when they were assimilated. Czechoslovakia became our protectorate. The move against Poland was purely a defensive one. We had no wish for war. It was the governments of Britain, Australia, New Zealand, India, and France who declared war on us. What were we to do but fight back?"

"You're crazy, just like Hitler. He was a madman, too. You saw what he did to all those Gypsies and Jews. He's probably killed millions of them," Brown said, a sharp edge in his tone.

"Propaganda. Yes, the undesirables had to be purged from poisoning our society. But they were simply moved to relocation camps," Phelps said.

"You're full of it. There're stories of gas chambers and furnaces. Millions dying from starvation, that's what the Third Reich is really all about," Brown said.

"Again, propaganda. You have prisons in America. I am sure conditions there are not the finest, either. We were separating ourselves as a people. Our only intent was for the Aryan race to prosper," Phelps said.

"By sending V-two rockets to Britain? Indiscriminately killing civilian men, women, and children?" Slick said.

"We were at war. A war declared on *us*," Phelps emphasized. "It strikes me as ironic that you Allies do the same but ignore the innocent lives taken."

"What do you mean?" Slick asked.

"Dresden," Phelps said, acting as if it pained him for the word to leave his lips. "I spoke with my cousin in late February. She was the only survivor from a family of five. Two weeks before, at night, the sirens started. Her family, along with the other one million members of the city, sought refuge in cellars or any place of safety. The bombs rolled in continuous thunder. Nonstop explosions devastated every building in their path. Fire, heat, smoke, no place was safe from the bombs and incendiaries that fell from the sky. The air was thick with dust, so hot it burned to breathe. They had to escape.

"Once outside, the horrors she described were unimaginable. The buildings were on fire and damaged. Vehicles and carts burned. People and horses cried in pain. Some had flames consuming their body as they ran. Even though all five in her family survived the first raid, three died immediately at the beginning of the second. In that raid, the bombs and incendiaries were bigger. The roads caught fire and became a molten trap for those traveling across it.

"Then the winds started. Air sucking from all around her to feed the column of flame growing at the center of the massive inferno. The vacuum created to feed the fiery storm stole my cousin's four-year-old daughter—ripping her tiny fingers from her desperate grasp. My cousin, too, might have suffered the same fate, save for two men who grabbed her at the last moment and pulled her to the safety of the Elbe River."

Phelps paused, and said, "Dresden was a cherished city, a cultural and historical treasure. The city possessed no military value, full of artists and craftsmen, and with no anti-aircraft defense. The Allies dare not judge themselves by the same measurement they judge the sons of Germany. My cousin tells me the number of dead is estimated at one-half million."

Phelps sounded like a man trying to justify his pursuit of a lost dream only to realize that pursuit cost him far more than he ever hoped to gain. He didn't seem to be an evil man. Brazo couldn't blame him for loving his country and didn't know why Dresden was hit so hard with the war in Europe so close to coming to an end. Mistakes were sure to be made by both sides. Dresden may not have been a mistake. History would have to be the judge of that.

"War is Hell," Jim Stone said.

"War does not determine who is right—only who is left," Brazo said. "Let's get some rest and hope the new day shows us a way out of here."

The men rubbed the wrinkles from their blankets and lay their bodies down, shifting against the earth underneath to find comfort.

CHAPTER 21

The boat drifted early morning on a lazy lake. Sugar-like snow sprinkled the mountain tops on the horizon. Erik watched as his father diligently waited for a fish to strike at his bait.

Turning his head, Christoph said, "You are not going to catch any fish if your hook does not go into the water."

Strangely, Erik felt like he was in a moment of time he had visited before. "I do not like to fish. I can fish all day and not catch anything. There are fish at the market. It seems it would be better to buy fish and use the time saved to do other things."

"Ah, you have always had a logical mind. You are missing out on important lessons in life if you only focus on end results."

"Lessons in life? What do you mean?"

"Erik, I know you do not like to fish. I insist on taking you to teach you things."

"It did not take me long to learn how to wind fishing line on a spool and how to bait a hook. Luring fish is more difficult, but there is little to learn about fishing."

Christoph smiled in a way he always did when he was about to give instruction. "When we go fishing, it is not about catching fish."

Erik thought that was one of the stupidest things to ever come out of his father's mouth. "We fish for *fish*. How is it not about catching fish?"

"Fishing, like life, is about the process. You are young, and youth tends to want an immediate reward. The seeds of wisdom are slow growing. The first lesson that fishing teaches is patience. A philosopher once said, *all things come to he who waits*. Patience is not one of your gifts in life. Learning to fish—spending the time to choose the proper bait, tying a knot to keep the hook secure, and tricking the fish into taking the bait teaches that rewards in life come from patience and commitment. Do you understand?"

He did, thinking back on his father's efforts and the big fish he watched him catch over the years. "What other life lessons does fishing teach beside patience?"

"Fishing teaches you to be resourceful. If one bait does not work, you must try another. You must use reasoning—the time of day, the time of the year, the weather around you, all factor in. Catching fish, like hunting, also teaches you to be self-sufficient. You can feed yourself and your family. Do you see how you can apply these steps to other challenges that you find in life?"

"Yes, I think so."

"With fishing, you can be alone with your thoughts. Contemplate your position in the universe. Commune with nature in solitude. Or, you can fish with others, strengthen the bond of friendship. You do know why we release fish that are too small to keep?"

"Yes, so that they will grow bigger to catch another day."

"If you were starving, you would eat a fish of any size. If the situation allows, then you make investments for the future. You must treat any business you deal with like an investment. Your schooling is an investment. The knowledge that you learn will one day be applied to a job that will pay you wages. The more you learn, the greater wages you will earn. Whereas learning in life never stops, it is important that your foundation is developed in your youth. Be all you can be, my son. Do not let life's distractions or the interference of others steer you away from your objectives."

Erik felt like the walls he had built around life had fallen, and a whole new world was open before him. It was as if he now saw life through his father's eyes.

"The day will come when you will be a man. I will not be on this Earth forever. I only want to help you become the best man you can be. Erik, son, I love you."

"I love you too, Father."

"Just wait until you get a little older," Christoph said, a sly smile growing across his lips. "You will learn how to lure the girls into your arms like a hungry fish."

Erik giggled at the thought of dropping a line and hook next Lina Engels, a schoolmate with long golden curls.

"Goodbye, my son." Christoph's smile faded, and his expression went blank.

Confused, Erik said, "Goodbye? But—" His father disappeared in a blink. Erik reached out into empty air and frantically looked about. The water was calm, but his father was gone, like he had never been there.

Something tapped him on the shoulder, and his mind pulled him from the dream back to reality.

*

"Erik...wake up, son."

The fog of sleep lifted, and Erik became aware of the early glow of dawn. At first, he had thought his father had spoken to him—because he heard the word *son*. But the voice was not his father's, and the words spoken in native English.

Christoph was lying next to him. Erik reached over and touched his father's hand. The hand felt strangely cool and the fingers stiff.

"Erik?"

The boy turned and saw the man called *Stone* sitting by his side, his hand resting on Erik's left shoulder.

"Your dad...your father passed away last night," Stone said. "I'm sorry."

His elbows on the blanket, he slowly propped himself up. His father looked like he was resting, with eyes closed, and a peaceful expression on his face. At first, Erik almost cried out in denial, but then a moment from his dream called back to him. *I will not be on this Earth forever.*

Erik knew his father would die one day. Everyone dies, but he did not expect to lose his father now, not like this.

"It happened just a few minutes ago. He...stopped breathing. I don't believe he suffered. That's something to be thankful for," Stone said.

Seeing his father with life no longer flowing through him was surreal. The body reminded him of a wax figure with a distinct separation of those of the living. Erik wondered now about the mysterious force called *life* and how it energized the human shell. But he would have to pursue his curiosities later.

He was alone. His mother and father, gone.

The day will come when you will be a man, his father had said in the dream.

Goodbye, my son.

"Goodbye, Father," Erik said softly and wiped a tear forming in his left eye.

"We'll bury him, and I'll say a few words to honor his memory, if that's okay," Stone said.

"I would like that," Erik said. "I will find something to make a marker." The boy rose and worked out the soreness in his body sleeping on the ground had brought. Giving one last look before he ventured forth, he thought, *that is just a body. My father is no longer there.*

*

Captain Brazo did his best to keep the remaining crew focused. He, Slick, and Phelps helped Jim Stone bury the commander. The other four crewmen kept their distance and didn't attend the short ceremony afterward. He couldn't blame his men. Giving homage to the enemy border-lined treason in some minds. If it wouldn't have been for the boy, Erik, Christoph would have been left to feed the scavengers. Not out of spite, but because resources, and energy was a resource, had to be conserved.

Erik had shown little emotion at the ceremony. Brazo thought if his father had died and he was the age of Erik, that he would have cried like a baby. Perhaps the tumultuous conditions in Europe over the years had hardened the youths. Erik did seem to lack a certain innocence American boys displayed. There was no telling what Hitler had done to brainwash the populace.

Artur Phelps didn't initiate conversation and kept his distance from the Americans. Maybe he was afraid to start an argument that might get out of control. Being the only U-boat crewman and allowed to carry a weapon was a privilege he was sure not to jeopardize.

Jim Stone shadowed Erik the last two hours as the survivors hiked to the peak of the high point.

The faint smell of briny ocean air invigorated Brazo's nostrils as they neared the top. He wasn't sure what was on the other side and didn't expect much. Looking out from higher ground gave them no advantage at this point. In any direction, the land looked essentially the same. Trees and foliage. Hills, mountains in the distance, flatlands, but nothing resembling civilization. No skyscrapers, smokestacks, or primitive villages cleared among the jungle. They were going to reach the last mission he had created to offer hope, and then what? Find nothing but an endless open sea? What do they do then? Turn around and head back down? Go where? Find the next pack of hungry dinosaurs, sprinkle salt all over themselves, and say, *come and get it*?

Rodrigue and Wallace were the first to reach the summit. Brazo watched their heads turn from side to side, but nothing caught their attention enough for them to show excitement. He wasn't surprised and felt stupid for feeling somewhat disappointed. There was no Santa Claus, Easter Bunny, or Tooth Fairy. There wouldn't be a way off this accursed place either.

Alan Slick came to his side as the rest of the group caught up with Rodrigue and Wallace. The terrain sloped downward near the same pitch as the side they had climbed, all the way to the ocean. The coast below them had a *U*-shaped indention. But as Brazo looked out to sea, a group of greenish clouds hovering above the water had his eyes widening.

"Is that what I think it is?" Brazo said.

Slick paused, and said, "It sure looks like it."

The storm that had brought them here, or one like it, it was there, not far away at all. Could it bring them back to 1945? Was this another wild hope induced by the madness of the situation? *There was no Santa Claus!* he reminded himself. But maybe, maybe this would be a one in a million chance to make it back to their time.

"Is that the storm that took us from our time?" Adam Rodrigue asked.

"Can't be sure," Brazo said.

"So what? It's already done its damage," Bob Brown said.

"The captain and I think that if the storm had the power to bring us here, it might have the power to bring us back home," Slick said.

"That true, Captain?" Bill Sanders said, his big, puppy dog eyes searched for a thread of hope to grasp.

"You can call it a hunch. You can call it wishful thinking. I could prove to be the biggest fool that ever lived," he said and shrugged. "If I have to choose between waiting in this land to become food in a dinosaur's stomach, or taking a chance of the storm bringing us back home, I'm going for the later."

"Do you think the storm might move over here to land?" Hampton Wallace asked.

"Unknown. We aren't sure how long that thing out there is going to last, either," Brazo said.

"Hmm, lot of good that's going to do us," Brown said. "It's going to take hours for us to get down to shore, and then what? Swim the mile or so to it? We'll all get eaten or drown way before we get to it. Even if we make it that far, it's just a storm. We'll be out there treading water for nothing."

"You're welcome to stay behind," Brazo said. He looked about. "We need to build a raft and try and make our way to it. If anyone doesn't want to take the risk, you are most welcome to stay here."

"I ain't staying here," Rodrigue said.

"Me neither," Wallace said.

"I will go," Phelps said.

Brown shot Phelps a scowl.

"Look at the ocean! It's falling," Erik said. The boy had been gazing toward the water.

Brazo had assumed Erik was lost in thought, grieving over his dad's death. Sure enough, though, the tide was moving out. Rapidly!

"Look at that," Slick said, and his bottom jaw sagged.

A dead tree floating near the coast rushed from the shoreline toward the green storm at sea. The water level drained while they were watching, almost as if someone had pulled the plug in a bathroom tub. Brazo estimated that the shoreline had moved fifty feet when the low tide rolled out!

"Unbelievable. I've never seen the tide move so quick and the water level drop that much," Brazo said.

"Captain, if we can build rafts by morning, we can wait for the tide to go out and ride toward the storm," Slick said.

Yes. An unimaginable opportunity had presented itself. Brazo looked up to the sky, hoping to find some confirmation that the Almighty had a plan, and all they had to do was seize upon it. But only the greenish fog beckoned below, with electrical sprites and fairies dancing in the mist.

"A gambling man wouldn't take the odds of our survival," Brazo said. "But a desperate man will take desperate measures to save his life and the lives of others. Men, this may be our last hurrah, so we'll have to give it all that we've got."

"What does *last hurrah* mean?" Phelps asked.

"It means that the attempt to reach the storm might be the last thing we ever do on this Earth," Slick said.

"Ah, yes. This may be our *last hurrah*," Phelps said. "I will do all that I can for us to be successful."

"I hope you make it there with us, buddy," Brown said, his compassion totally out of character.

Phelps gave him a wary eye.

"Because I can't wait until you get a firsthand look at a United States prison from the inside. Bread and water. Water and bread. God bless America," Brown said and then smirked.

"Brown, shut your trap. We're all in this together, right now," Brazo said.

"Yes, sir," Brown said and lowered his head.

"Okay, men, the trip will be easier because it's all downhill. Watch your step and watch out for each other," Brazo said, capturing Brown's gaze. "Erik, stay close to Stone. Let's go."

*

Artur Phelps held the two pieces of bamboo securely as Slick tied a clove hitch knot. From there, the XO carefully wrapped the rope around a cross join, going over and under—and keeping the rope tight.

The two had just begun the base construction of the second raft. The captain had insisted on cutting the bamboo. The other crewmen were on watch or gathering materials.

"That is a nice knot you tie," Phelps said. "Have you built rafts before?"

"A long time ago, back when I was a kid. I spent every spare moment I could on or by the water," Slick said. "I even carved a boat out of a fallen tree one time. It took me two months, but it floated just fine."

Something had been weighing on the XO's mind ever since Phelps made his comment about the Aryan race. He tried to let it go and not cause any conflict. But the longer they worked together, the more pronounced his agitation had become. "Phelps, last night, you said something. How you are part of the Aryan race and how you wanted to be a separate people. Do you really believe that one breed of people is inherently superior to others?"

"There are many primitive people in the world. Do you not believe that you are their superior?"

"Well, I guess you could say that I feel superior to uneducated people—like Bush People living in grass huts with dirt floors. But people of any race can be educated. Humans are equal like that."

"But a pure line of breeding can produce superior men and women. You breed animals in the United States in order to create the finest specimens. Why should we not breed people?"

"Are you serious? People aren't like animals. Men and women meet and fall in love. Having children is a blend of their love. A factory might be able to spit out blond hair, blue-eyed dolls, but men and women should never be used as factories," Slick said. "Another thing, the Jews have lived in Germany for centuries. How is the so-called Aryan race heritage any greater than theirs?"

"The Jews held to their religious ways, separating them from us. Jewish bankers enslaved the people of Germany. The Aryan race is superior to any other. Hitler had a solution, and the people followed his leadership," Phelps said.

"It's not all as black and white as you make it sound," Slick said, tying the last knot. He then took his knife and cut the rope.

"What do you mean?"

"Jews and Aryans have lived amongst each other for years. You know, my mother is from Germany. Came over to the States before the Great War."

"How would I know that?"

"Sorry," Slick said and smirked. "That's how Americans talk sometime. But yes, my mother did come over here. That makes me half German."

Phelps cocked his head to the side, and said, "What is your point?"

"You know what else? Her maiden name was *Phelps*."

The German narrowed his eyes. "Is that true?"

"Oh yes, it most certainly is true. Say, do you think we might be related?" Slick asked.

"Many people share my last name who are not related to me."

"I'm sure. She was from Heidelberg. Do you have family in *Heidelberg*?"

Phelps' eyes widened. He paused, and said, "I do."

"See, we might be cousins. You and me."

"There is no way for us to know. Again, what is your point?"

"Point? We're from two different countries with vastly different beliefs, yet we just might share the same genetics."

"And?" Phelps let the word hang in the air.

"And, there's something else I didn't tell you about my mother," Slick said, his gaze locked on Phelps'. "She's a Jew. That makes me half-Jewish. Oh wait, I'm sure to you that there is no such thing as a *half-Jew*. I'm Jewish."

Phelps shrugged, obviously wanting to avoid escalating conflict.

"You see? Look, look at my nose." Slick turned his head so Phelps could view his profile. "See how it hooks a bit. You know, a Jew nose you Germans stereotype in your propaganda?"

"Races had different characteristics," Phelps said.

"They do," Slick said agreeably. "But haven't you noticed when you look in the mirror that your nose *hooks* the same way as mine?"

"It does not."

"Are you blind?" Slick said, realizing the growing anger in his voice. He gritted his back teeth together, and said, "Okay, Phelps. I'll let it go. Don't worry, your secret is safe with me. Now, let's move on to the next cross join, and I'll start tying it up."

Artur Phelps kept his lips tight. A bead of sweat rolled down his cheek.

*

The hatchet Brazo used to chop the eight-inch-in-diameter bamboo dulled with each swing. At first, cutting bamboo to length had gone quickly. Now, it took four times as long. Unfortunately, they had brought only that one hatchet. Brazo considered going to the water's edge and try to sharpen the blade on a flat stone. But, they nearly had enough to finish the second raft, so he decided to sweat it out until the job was complete.

Fearing that the storm hovering offshore would move out to sea, the captain found himself looking over his shoulder toward it every couple of minutes. Each time his heart skipped a bit seeing it there, praying to whoever would listen for the chance for it to remain.

Brazo had never felt this much anxiety before in his life. He tried to calm himself; they were still eighteen hours away from the first low tide tomorrow. There was no guarantee the storm would be there eighteen seconds from now, and each second ticked off in his mind felt like an hour. They were so close at a chance. He didn't know why, but something inside made him think they could actually make it. Was that some human condition influencing his rational mind? To come this far to fail would seem to be the cruelest joke the universe could pull on them.

The captain cut another piece of bamboo, leaving a foot of stump poking up. He let the hatchet fall to the ground and massaged his right hand with his left. Arching his back, and wiping the sweat from his brow with a forearm, he saw Erik staring at him a few feet away.

Brazo gazed back, but the boy didn't say a word. He didn't know what was up, but something was definitely on Erik's mind. "Erik, are you okay?" Brazo asked.

Erik nodded but remained silent.

"Look, I know you must feel real bad about losing your dad. I don't know what to say to make it better. I do know that time has a way of healing. But you're going through the worst of it now. All I can do is say *I'm sorry*, and if you need to talk to someone, I'm here for you."

"I do want to talk, but not about my father," Erik said.

"Okay, let's talk." Brazo stepped over by the boy.

"The U-boat was on its way to South America. Aboard, there were high-ranking officials who were with the SS. I once heard them speaking about the war. They did not know I was listening. There are things they said which could cause many more people to die. I do not want to betray my country, but I know that we have lost the war. Something inside me does not want to see other people die. I am tired of the killing. I want the world to be in peace."

"Wars end in treaties. Peace will eventually come. I don't know what Germany's future will be. The United States is a fair nation. You don't have to worry about the German people becoming slaves of the Allies. Tell me, what did you overhear?"

"The SS agents, Barbie, Eichmann, Mengele, Stangl, and a man and wife who called themselves Viktor. Even though they knew Germany was about to fall, there was still a plan to deliver an atomic bomb to Japan."

Brazo raised a hand. "Wait. You're telling me Klaus Barbie, Dr. Mengele, Eichmann and Stangl were on the U-boat? I had no idea those high-ranking officials had slipped past us."

"Yes. We were all to get papers in South America and begin new lives."

"And you're saying the Japanese might get ahold of an atomic bomb? I need to hear every detail you can remember of the conversation," Brazo said.

"It is even worse than that. There is an attack planned in the United States."

"What kind of attack?"

"A ship named *John Carver* is to arrive two days from the time the storm brought us here, somewhere near New York City. There is an atomic bomb on the ship. Another ship, the *Black Point*, also has an atomic bomb on board and will go up the Potomac River to DC. The bombs will be detonated at the same time in hopes of destroying your government."

Could this be true? Brazo didn't believe the boy had it in him to invent this wild tale all on his own. Did the German's really have the bomb? The story seemed impossible, but the impossible had become the norm of late. "Is there anything else you can tell me about the bombs in the States?"

"That is all I overheard. A U-boat is on its way to Japan to deliver a complete atomic bomb, plans, and materials to build three more. The number of the boat is *U-234*," Erik said.

Brazo took a deep breath and chewed on his bottom lip. Blowing up New York City and Washington, DC, might very well cripple the United States. If Japan had the bomb, well, then there was probably no way the US could win the war. Of all the events Brazo had gone through the last couple of days, this scenario was by far the scariest. "You said the bombs in the US were supposed to go off two days after the storm took us here? It may be too late to stop it."

"Yes, Frank Viktor said in *two days*."

"Viktor…Viktor. I don't recognize the name."

Erik hesitated a bit, and then said, "I do not believe that was his real name. What I can say, is that when I overheard the conversation, I thought it was the Führer himself speaking."

The boy's words hit Brazo like a sucker punch. Hitler? Alive and on a U-boat to South America? Surely, Erik was wrong. Hitler was dead. Or was he? Even if all that Erik had told him had a one percent possibility of being true, getting back to their time was now exponentially more important.

"Erik, what you told me could save many lives. Maybe millions of lives, if we can make it back. You did right by telling me, and you didn't betray your country. The best thing for all is for the war to end now."

Erik nodded and looked at the ground.

"Let's get this bamboo over to the others and finish the second raft," Brazo said.

The boy stepped over to one end of the bamboo and lifted it.

The captain grabbed the other end and led the way. Slick needed to hear the details as soon as possible. One of them had to survive and convince the Navy brass of the impending doom.

CHAPTER 22

Because high and low tide shifted every six hours, Brazo and the survivors witnessed the maddening rush of water onto the coastland and back out before the next morning. He knew the ocean's tides were affected by the sun, moon, and rotation of the Earth, but had no explanation why the tides flowed in and out so quickly. Was this phenomenon only present here on this particular coast? Did the storm directly out to sea contribute in any way? Questions, but no answers, not that it mattered, anyway.

It neared time for the tide to roll out. Brazo, Slick, Erik, and Stone were aboard one raft. Brown, Wallace, Rodrigue, Sanders, and Phelps, the other. Each had crude paddles that would take a lot of extra effort to navigate the waters. The paddles were at least superior to the stocks of M1 rifles, of which only two were carried aboard each raft. Space was at a premium; bringing more rifles would have cluttered the seating arrangement. If they encountered any prehistoric sea creatures as before, they would have to make do with minimal firepower. At least they each had their Colt .45s. Judging from the dead tree that was caught up in the tide yesterday, the ride out to sea to the storm would be fairly quick. It wouldn't take long for them to find out if a miracle could come true or if they had the made worst and final mistake of their lives.

"Just believe, Captain. Just believe," Jim Stone said.

His reverie broke at Stone's words of encouragement. Truthfully, he didn't think believing in an outcome would have any power influencing reality. Still, he did remember the Bible stories involving faith. If he expected any less than succeeding, then he might fall short of accomplishing his goal.

"It's almost time, Captain," Slick said while looking at his watch.

"Wallace, keep your men focused over there," the Captain called out.

"Yes, sir," Wallace said.

Something seemed to grab hold underneath the raft and began to pull it forward, slowly at first, and the top of the water appeared undisturbed. The men on the rafts, on their knees and bracing themselves, held onto the paddles as the outgoing tide pulled them away.

Brazo watched the ocean leave the shoreline, exposing wet sand and stranding small, strange-looking fish. The wind blew his face and nearly took his cap off. He wasn't sure how fast they were moving, but the only other time he had traveled like this was on the Arkansas River taking a white water rapid ride.

All was going to plan. The other raft traveled just a little behind, about twenty feet across from them. Both rafts careened toward the storm, its green mist and eerie billowing clouds loomed before them with its mouth opened wide. It's mysterious electrical field energized the air, and Brazo felt its sprites crawling over his skin.

Something large and black briefly rose in the water between the two rafts and submerged just as fast. The fast moving objects had apparently piqued the interest of some prehistoric creature. Not now! Not when they were so close.

A gray mass surfaced alongside Brazo's raft. Jutting up from the water, a long neck carried a narrow head with sharp teeth straight toward Erik.

Jim Stone swung his paddle, knocking the beast on the side of its mouth. It snorted in pain and thrashed its head back at its attacker. Stone didn't have time to block the incoming missile. Instead, his right shoulder took the brunt of the blow, knocking him head-first into the water.

"Jim!" Slick yelled and crawled to the back of the raft, searching for the man overboard.

The beast hung back and headed where its prey had fallen.

Just like that, another man's life was lost. The captain was powerless to do anything now but pay the consequences of his decision.

The back of the second raft lifted out of the water, sending Phelps, Brown, and Sanders into the air. Wallace and Rodrigue slid off the front, plunging into the ocean, with the empty raft racing over them. The water boiled with two large black masses engaged in a feeding frenzy. Crocodile-like mouths snapped and chewed as men screamed out in pain.

Gone. Five men who had lived through more in the last few days than most ordinary people would in ten lifetimes, their lives brought to a brutal end.

The green mist grew thick, blocking the captain's view of the carnage. They neared the belly of the storm now.

Erik held on dearly to the raft.

Slick had his paddle at the ready, for what little good it may have to offer.

By now, the fog was so thick it weighed heavy in Brazo's nostrils. He felt it invade his lungs. The mist enveloped his body, becoming like he wore it as a second skin. He could no longer see Slick or Erik. The green fog became his only reality. Suddenly, he felt weightless. His head swooned, and his body plunged into what felt like a bottomless pit.

Brazo was being eaten alive by the electrical monster. One atom at a time pulled away from his body. The voracious beast showed no mercy and mocked the captain for having the audacity to think he could manipulate the electrical God to do his bidding.

T.W. Brazo felt his connection to humanity drift away. With each second, loneliness, as if a young child separated from his mother, grew in intensity. His soul slowly emptied from his body. All that he had endured in life, all that he held precious, seemed so insignificant now. His fate no longer rested with his decisions. That brought peace upon him like he had never felt before.

He was tired. It was time to rest. It was a well-deserved rest. One that he felt would last an eternity.

CHAPTER 23

Captain Brazo became aware as he looked through a pair of binoculars on a bright and sunny day. He dropped the binoculars to his chest and looked hurriedly about. He was on the observation deck of a ship. The wind blew calmly. The smell of the salty ocean spray invigorated his inner being. This was the crow's nest of the *USS Sutton*!

"Captain!" XO Alan Slick cried with glee as he stepped from the top of the ladder onto the observation deck. "Captain, we're back!"

"It's true," Brazo said in awe. "It's true! We've come back." His smile melted as his mind flooded with the news that the German boy had given him of the upcoming attack. "Slick, what day is this?"

"I...don't know. I just found myself on the ladder moments ago," Slick said.

Brazo called down to a crewman working on deck. "Sailor, what day is it?"

The young man looked up. It was Adam Rodrigue. "Uh, Friday, sir."

Brazo wasn't interested in the day. He wanted the date, but that could wait. "Rodrigue! Are you okay?" Brazo said. After just witnessing the man's death, it was sort of a shock to see him alive and apparently well.

"Yes, Captain. Fit as a fiddle."

"Where were you yesterday?"

Wariness in his voice, as if he didn't understand the question, Rodrigue said, "Right here on deck, doing my daily duties, sir."

Brazo lowered his voice and told the XO, "He doesn't remember. He died back there, so he doesn't remember. We lived. That's why we remember."

Recalling the storm that started it all, Brazo hurried to the other side of the observation deck. Just as before, the walls of green clouds brewed in the distance.

The captain went to the radio and picked up the mic. "Stone, talk to me."

"Yes, Captain," Jim Stone said.

"Today's date, what is it?"

"It's the fourth, sir."

Brazo turned to Slick. "We're back right where it started. We've been given a second chance." A smile grew across his lips wide enough to show teeth.

"How is that even possible?" Slick said.

"I don't know, and right now, I don't care," Brazo said, ending the celebration and returning to the business at hand. "We've got to go back and make sure those atomic bombs don't reach New York City and DC. That U-boat delivery to Japan has to be stopped, too."

"Captain," the radio squawked.

"Go ahead."

"Radar's picked up a bogey two miles starboard. We suspect it's a periscope."

"There it is. This is where we made the mistake the first time," Brazo said. "I'll be damned if I allow that to happen again. I don't care who is aboard that U-boat." He squeezed the mic, and said, "I'm suspending the *Sutton's* shakedown. These are my orders, take the ship immediately back to base. Is that clear?"

"Yes sir, Captain. Loud and clear."

Brazo shook his head. "I don't know how to quite figure all of this."

"What do you mean?" Slick asked.

"If we hadn't gone after the U-boat in the first place, then we would never know about the upcoming German sneak attack. But now that we aren't going after it, we have a chance to prevent it. It all seems so...predestined, in some sort of way."

"They do say the Lord works in mysterious ways," Slick said.

"That they do. If I've learned nothing else these past few days, it's that I'm not privileged enough to understand the mind of God," Brazo said.

"You're in good company, Captain. No one can. Maybe that's the whole point of life. Each person's individual struggle to understand the mind of God," Slick said.

"Right now, I'll have to leave that to philosophers. I've got a job to do. Nothing else matters, and I will not rest until it's complete."

***

Erik Neuzetser became aware from inside the command room of *U-616*. His father, Christoph Neuzetser, the commander, pressed his face to the periscope. Water dripped from a flange, wetting the floor under his feet.

His father was alive! Alive!

Erik's mind raced with the events of the last few days but was pulled back by the normalcy of current reality. Did any of those horrors really happen, or was it some type of dream?

The last thought he had before now was drowning in the green fog, and then fading off to sleep.

He suddenly realized he had lived this moment before. This was when Captain Brazo's ship turned to engage the U-boat. Would he do it again this time? Did the Captain, too, remember the storm that took them back in time? Would Brazo attack, and the storm take them to the prehistoric land to repeat the same events?

Then Erik questioned if he had died in the green storm. Was this his eternal reward? Reliving the last three days over and over. Caught in some hellish loop that would never end?

"The Destroyer, it is turning," Christoph said.

"Has it spotted us, Commander?" Lieutenant Bach asked.

"I do not think so. The ship is veering away from us and appears to be heading toward the mainland," Christoph said.

Erik breathed a sigh of relief. The captain must have remembered the great danger his country was in. Chasing after a handful of SS agents and Adolph Hitler himself wasn't worth the destruction of the two most important cities in the United States.

It was time for Erik to take control of his life and no longer be like a leaf caught in the wind, blown about by the whims and desires of others. He trotted out of the command room. Less than a minute later, he returned with a tool bag in his hand.

Christoph turned to his son. "Erik, fetch—"

"I have the tool bag, Father. I will use a wrench to tighten the flange," Erik said.

The commander looked dumfounded, which was an expression seldom seen on his father's face. "Erik, that is a good boy. You make your father proud."

Erik smiled to himself as he searched for the proper wrench. Witnessing his father's death the day before seemed like a dream. A nightmare. He didn't know how or why, but the storm had taken him back to his own time. It was useless now to try and make sense of it all.

"When I get finished here, I will go to the sick bay and see if I can help Dr. Mengele care for the Viktors," Erik said.

The commander looked even more taken aback. "Yes, that would be a fine thing for you to do." A satisfied smile crossed his lips.

It warmed Erik's heart to have his father again. Still, he was his own man inside and would not compromise his beliefs for anyone. That said, he would learn life's lessons and build a strong foundation. In hopes of one day of becoming wiser than his father.

The question still remained of the fate of the crew once South America was reached. Was there a plot to kill all the crewmen so that *Viktor* and the SS agents did not have to fear betrayal?

Erik believed there was only one way to assure their safety. He would make an opportunity to take two pills out of that cobalt blue glass bottle. The cyanide would find its way into the mouths of both Frank Viktor and his wife. With the Führer out of the way, the other SS agents would be forced into anonymity, with no hopes of continuing the war.

He would ask his father if they would adopt the German Shepard, Blondi. The dog would need to start a new life, too, and Erik needed a new best friend to start life over with.

Epilogue

U-234 fled across the ocean for Japan. T.W. Brazo, Captain of the *USS Sutton*, followed.

THE END

COMING IN 2017: PREHISTORIC WWII: PACIFIC

CHECK OUT OTHER GREAT DINOSAUR THRILLERS

LOST WORLD OF PATAGONIA
by Dane Hatchell

An earthquake opens a path to a land hidden for millions of years. Under the guise of finding cryptid animals, Ace Corporation sends Alex Klasse, a Cryptozoologist and university professor, his associates, and a band of mercenaries to explore the Lost World of Patagonia. The crew boards a nuclear powered All-Terrain Tracked Carrier and takes a harrowing ride into the unknown.

The expedition soon discovers prehistoric creatures still exist. But the dangers won't prevent a sub-team from leaving the group in search of rare jewels. Tensions run high as personalities clash, and man proves to be just as deadly as the dinosaurs that roam the countryside.

Lost World of Patagonia is a prehistoric thriller filled with murder, mayhem, and savage dinosaur action.

SAVAGE ISLAND
by Alan Spencer

Somewhere in the Atlantic Ocean, an uncharted island has been used for the illegal dumping of chemicals and pollutants for years by Globo Corp's. Private investigator Pierce Range will learn plenty about the evil conglomerate when Susan Branch, an environmentalist from The Green Project, hires him to join the expedition to save her kidnapped father from Globo Corp's evil hands.

Things go to hell in a hurry once the team reaches the island. The bloodthirsty dinosaurs and voracious cannibals are only the beginning of the fight for survival. Pierce must unlock the mysteries surrounding the toxic operation and somehow remain in one piece to complete the rescue mission.

Ratchet up the body count, because this mission will leave the killing floor soaked in blood and chewed up corpses. When the insane battle ends, will there by anybody left alive to survive Savage Island?

CHECK OUT OTHER GREAT DINOSAUR THRILLERS

THE VALLEY
by **Rick Jones**

In a dystopian future, a self-contained valley in Argentina serves as the 'far arena' for those convicted of a crime. Inside the Valley: carnivorous dinosaurs generated from preserved DNA. The goal: cross the Valley to get to the Gates of Freedom. The chance of survival: no one has ever completed the journey. Convicted of crimes with little or no merit, Ben Peyton and others must battle their way across fields filled with the world's deadliest apex predators in order to reach salvation. All the while the journey is caught on cameras and broadcast to the world as a reality show, the deaths and killings real, the macabre appetite of the audience needing to be satiated as Ben Peyton leads his team to escape not only from a legal system that's more interested in entertainment than in justice, but also from the predators of the Valley.

JURASSIC DEAD
by **Rick Chesler & David Sakmyster**

An Antarctic research team hoping to study microbial organisms in an underground lake discovers something far more amazing: perfectly preserved dinosaur corpses. After one thaws and wakes ravenously hungry, it becomes apparent that death, like life, will find a way.
Environmental activist Alex Ramirez, son of the expedition's paleontologist, came to Antarctica to defend the organisms from extinction, but soon learns that it is the human race that needs protecting.

SEVEREDPRESS

CHECK OUT OTHER GREAT DINOSAUR THRILLERS

WRITTEN IN STONE
by David Rhodes

Charles Dawson is trapped 100 million years in the past. Trying to survive from day to day in a world of dinosaurs he devises a plan to change his fate. As he begins to write messages in the soft mud of a nearby stream, he can only hope they will be found by someone who can stop his time travel. Professor Ron Fontana and Professor Ray Taggit, scientists with opposing views, each discover the fossilized messages. While attempting to save Charles, Professor Fontana, his daughter Lauren and their friend Danny are forced to join Taggit and his group of mercenaries. Taggit does not intend to rescue Charles Dawson, but to force Dawson to travel back in time to gather samples for Taggit's fame and fortune. As the two groups jump through time they find they must work together to make it back alive as this fast-paced thriller climaxes at the very moment the age of dinosaurs is ending.

HARD TIME
by Alex Laybourne

Rookie officer Peter Malone and his heavily armed team are sent on a deadly mission to extract a dangerous criminal from a classified prison world. A Kruger Correctional facility where only the hardest, most vicious criminals are sent to fend for themselves, never to return.

But when the team come face to face with ancient beasts from a lost world, their mission is changed. The new objective: Survive.

CHECK OUT OTHER GREAT DINOSAUR THRILLERS

SPINOSAURUS
by Hugo Navikov

Brett Russell is a hunter of the rarest game. His targets are cryptids, animals denied by science. But they are well known by those living on the edges of civilization, where monsters attack and devour their animals and children and lay ruin to their shantytowns.

When a shadowy organization sends Brett to the Congo in search of the legendary dinosaur cryptid Kasai Rex, he will face much more than a terrifying monster from the past. Spinosaurus is a dinosaur thriller packed with intrigue, action and giant prehistoric predators.

LAND OF DEATH
by Eric S Brown & Alex Laybourne

A group of American soldiers, fleeing an organized attack on their base camp in the Middle East, encounter a storm unlike anything they've seen before. When the storm subsides, they wake up to find themselves no longer in the desert and perhaps not even on Earth. The jungle they've been deposited in is a place ruled by prehistoric creatures long extinct. Each day is a struggle to survive as their ammo begins to run low and virtually everything they encounter, in this land they've been hurled into, is a deadly threat.